Imaginary Epics
From the Cosmos

Bacteria, The Good, The Bad, The Ugly

Tales of Myths and Fantasy

Around The World on Three Underwear

Six Decades To Wisdom…..(maybe)

Sonnets of a Human Soul – a book of Poems

A Collection of Fables & Tales

Diagnosis

IMAGINARY EPICS
FROM THE COSMOS

Adventurous Science Fiction Stories

Darryl Leslie Gopaul

iUniverse, Inc.
New York   Bloomington

Imaginary Epics From the Cosmos
Adventurous Science Fiction Stories

iUniverse books may be ordered through booksellers or by contacting:

iUniverse
1663 Liberty Drive
Bloomington, IN 47403
www.iuniverse.com
1-800-Authors (1-800-288-4677)

ISBN: 978-1-4502-3599-0 (pbk)
ISBN: 978-1-4502-3600-3 (ebk)

Printed in the United States of America

iUniverse rev. date: 6/25/10

CONTENTS

DEDICATION:

This work is dedicated to Tanya & Laura, to Daphne,
to Karl and Roberta our link to Austria.

EARTH HAS AN INTRUDER

INTRODUCTION

Earth Has an Intruder: Unlike anything earthlings would have expected. It came from the deep reaches of the cosmos. This intruder is not seeking power, domination or even contact with humans. It arrives as a small moon, orbits around earth balancing the gravitational pulls of the sun and earth's moon.

Welcome to stories from the cosmos where there are threats to mankind but of a natural type just the passing of an unusual moon-like body. It could be the sword of Damocles.

MATTER DOES NOT STAND ALONE IN THE PHYSICS OF THE COSMOS

Just as the Big Bang gave the Cosmos some structure and form, it also shows when there is lack of order or a bad design fit, by simply destroying and remaking parts of the universe. The Laws of the Cosmos are also capable of designing a plan that supports and nurtures the parts that it wishes to maintain for it may be a physical fit necessary at that period of time. Another analogy would that be that, it must fit into God's plans of which Man is not made aware. Faith in God provides spiritual security and comfort to those who do not understand and to those who feel helpless with problems too big for their imagination and intellect.

The beauty of a Cosmos that was formed, either through the sciences of astrophysics or other forces, divine or sublime is that it enlightens and gives promise. Maybe 'God' is still watching over us in spite of ourselves. As the Cosmos is expanding, physical material from unbelievable powerful forces caused by imploding suns eventually form the phenomenon known as black holes. The outcome from this activity produces tremendous nuclear energies and this increases the need for Mankind to travel into outer space and to tap into this free unlimited energy source. The continuous movement of small bodies such as asteroids, smaller dwarf moons and planets come into their own right. The stew of the cosmos is dynamic, never sleeping, adding and subtracting but always keeping the energy in full force but in different forms. The nuclear energy that is in the deep cosmos is greater than anything that mankind can imagine. Millions or billions of megatons of nuclear energy more than man could create even in miniature on earth. This should be tapped into by Mankind for it will allow him to enter and travel the greater cosmos.

Technology development is at an increase at this time of the 21st century but there appears to be no rush to speed up the process. This will be Man's undoing for he still lacks the knowledge even though he observes the cosmos. Man has not learnt matters of the cosmos will never remain the same not for a second or a billion years. His temporary home, Earth has a limited shelf life. Man will be forced into making hard decisions for he is unprepared for depletion of the physical stores needed for his life form to exist. These stocks are all located in the planetary bodies found in deep space. He may even find himself up against other alien life forms that would need similar resources. Awake! Mankind you are under the scrutiny of time and change.

Background:

In the year 2009, Earth's scientists have confidently confirmed that the Cosmos was formed after the "Big Bang" approximately 10 billion years ago give or take a billion years. It is also suggested using man's concept of time that our third planet Earth came into being about 4 billion years give or take a half billion. The time of the Cosmos has nothing to do with the artificial time that man has created. Indeed, the concepts of time, space and distance as separate entities remain an imaginary game to our earthly scientists at least up until the middle of the twentieth century.

These men of science, however, have given Earth and its population a great deal to think about in the field of cosmology. There are billions of planets, suns and floating bodies in the great seemingly unending cosmos. There are massive nuclear explosions in outer space that release vast amounts of energy, gamma radiation and an array of other radiations all very malevolent to biological life forms such as Mankind. While the nearness of all this power can be traced to a simple atomic structure which for some reason had the need to explode or implode. Whichever it was, there was the development of space as we know it today. The major question is always why? Why did a simple atom change to become a major source of energy causing the expansion of space and time? A fundamental question still is why was it there to begin with?

This should make scientists weep into their telescopes for the concept of God the creator and ultimate provider begins to have credence in the development of religion. The scientific populations have not provided answers and have not come up with a negation of God therefore there is room for a religious philosophy to coexist with a scientific one. Speculation, however, is a vital part of Man's make up as is imagination and the power to day dream. The concept in physics to date reveals that the ultimate speed detected is the travel of light which works out to be around 186,000 miles per second. So the concept of speed has some foundation but what about the other two travel constants which are time and distance?

Hypothetically, when the Big Bang took place different galaxies were formed and different types of energy forms developed. The concept of different life forms becomes an indisputable scientific concept and possibility. It could also be deducted that the three concepts of time, distance and speed may have met on an even plain. There appears to be a celestial plan on how the tremendous radiations in outer space caused by massive energy outbursts assist in the forming and reforming of the physical elements in the universe. The explanation of the control and directional order remain elusive to mankind for all he sees is great chaos from his perspective and his limited lifespan.

The major reason for making these statements is founded on the concept of a scientific certainty and that is, *matter is neither created nor destroyed*. If that is an acceptable posture on Earth, then an experimental model is given to man, a carbon based life form, to study, thrive and develop the examples of the cosmos as presented to him in miniature on earth. This story begins with the concept that when the Big Bang occurred, there was a pattern and logic for its continuance. This celestial experiment is still at work and as a child made of a bit of stardust, humankind knows what is out there as this tale will reveal. Humans know because they are part of this cosmos and whether it is genetic or cosmos logic, the part knows the whole in some unexplained way. There is a reason for all these planets and celestial bodies that float in order in the Cosmos. Man is about to find out 5 million years later.

The Journey begins:

So it was over 5 billion years ago when the bodies of the cosmos were extruded into the medium now known as space that a small global body no bigger than Earth's own moon began on a journey. Knowing the hazards and the violence in the cosmos, it is difficult to understand how such a small body could travel unimpeded through the myriad of galaxies, flotillas of meteorites and space rocks particles and dynamic explosions of nuclear forces that cannot be calculated by any scientist, that were in its pathway. This little body is referred to as *Unis* and it passed through the forces of many a supernova, the pull of distant black holes and galaxies that were at least a few billion light years away from earth.

It seemingly moved with a focus bypassing all obstacles cataclysmic by any measure and moved in some direction in its sight. It inserted itself and became part of a small constellation of planets that surrounded a sun that was larger than Earth' sun but it occupied a distance relative to that of Pluto in Earth's solar system. When that sun began to wane, this little body was ejected from its orbit and was flung out of that system before the sun went super nova. This must have happened many times to *Unis* as it crossed millions if not billions of miles in the great outer regions of space. It moved away before the magnetic forces expanded from the dying sun. How it survived remains its mystery that only time and human scientific knowledge would be able to partially investigate in the future.

There must be many tiny bodies such as asteroids that float around in a similar fashion in the deep cosmos and one wonders how long it would take for them to escape. It is the supposition that their future if they are caught in the gravity of larger planets or suns they just crash for the greater force wins over the smaller mass. Others just disappear into black holes to be obliterated then regurgitated later in some different form of energy. Chances are this does indeed happen for scientists on earth have witnessed the impact of a huge comet that crashed onto the surface of Jupiter. When one observes the pock marked surface of our moon then it is safe to assume that great asteroid masses may be taken out of existence when they pass into the vicinity of the powerful black holes, stronger gravitational pulls of planets or near supernova stars. Their use being buried into the planets and suns where they land is still unknown.

A HEAVENLY SPHERE

The populations of earth were exposed to the news media every night as the spectacle of this fast moving comet-like body approaching their sun. The statisticians began to make gambles of how long it would take to get to Earth's solar system. Others did the calculations which showed that it would just fly past Earth with no consequence or peril. The vision of this small grey body traveling with increased speed towards the solar system brought out the end of the world "Doom-Sayers" The more progressive thinkers became philosophers, who tried to make some sober deductions. The world masses were told to calm down from the building hysteria that was beginning to affect the world populations and their governments.

Governments tried to keep control of their peoples and to give hope. In certain states a black out of information was attempted but there were so many ways of receiving information that even the most sophisticated black out attempts proved useless. It was also a time for the now almost forgotten religious bodies to come out into the open and to shout aloud that they were always correct. *God whom society had shunned was about to bring about Armageddon to the Earth as the scripture had foretold.* There was a boom in the upsurge of religions but again the old rivaling hostilities were revived even in such enlightened societies of the 22nd century. When all else failed, there was always the all dependable God, in whom even the keenest atheists began to have doubts for here was living proof that the end of mankind was at hand. Rational thinking went out the door as voodoo religions and science filled the gap that needed hope.

Politicians had to deal with massive numbers of suicides and sometimes that included whole families comprising of three of four generations. Indeed, there were many groups of humans that made the decisions to live in communes away from the material world. When they also saw the approaching body on a direct course entering the sun's gravity, they held a sermon of sorts and the whole population committed mass suicide. Young children as well as the aged were all killed at the thought of extinction by collision.

Early stages of panic:
With religions preaching prayer and forgiveness while asking their flock to prepare for death, governments began planning a survival strategy of sorts for themselves. These included retreating and hiding in deep mountain caverns and even using the deep undersea research laboratories as a way of getting away from immediate death that was fast approaching Earth. The plight of humans was pitiful for there were no plans for anyone even though there were a few hair brained schemes; paralysis of the known politicians had set in.

One of the schemes included that a small group of scientists and politicians should hide out in the Moon station. Others thought that a few should be going to Mars, which resulted in a long list of disasters when man eventually did get to the red planet. Essentially, running away to more hostile environment that was never equipped for long term habitation was one plan. It was literally running away from the fire into a cauldron. Others thought it a good idea to just take off on a flight and remain above the Earth's surface and land after the collision. There was no carrier that could carry thousands much less the millions of earthlings who if left behind would surely perish.

Little men think in little ways and salvation as it seems always remain, in the hands of little minds. A few social thinkers of an earlier century thought that Earth had indeed been visited by aliens from outer space. In fact it was thought that a shadow government may have been in charge globally for many years and had made the decision to let these aliens integrate into that of *Homo sapiens*. This was all back in the late nineteen sixties or late 20th century, when Earth had begun the very early stages of outer space exploration. Men even then could have conniptions just thinking of the colour of their fellow Earthmen. How much worse could it be if there were truly outer earth species trying to infiltrate into our societies and mate with our females on Earth?

Some of the cleverer writers thought that such hybrid humanoids may be useful in space exploration. Indeed, seeing some of earth's humans one often wondered whether they were from earth at all but this is physical satire. It was the early days of terrestrial isolationism for visiting the moon, then Mars meant that our days in being earth bound was at an end. It was just a matter of time before our female astronauts became pregnant and brought forth the next generation of human beings born on an extra terrestrial planet. Permanent bases went along with each landing on these neighboring planets in our solar system. The first mass movement had been tried back in the early part of the 21st century but there was a religious and ethical outcry demanding that the children be brought back to Earth and be raised as earthlings. What a waste for these children and their own offspring could have had the new skills and tolerance for outer space that would have benefited earth's human population.

The whole program was cut back because there were no outward thought of the needs of Earth at the time. Many just saw local earthly needs as some emotional discomfort and the decision to stop building communities in outer space was taken for a very simplistic reason. The moon was closer and if there was a problem then it was easy, relatively speaking, to rescue our humans. However Mars was further away approximately 35 million miles and so with the rockets available at the time it would not be possible to bring back anyone in time from any disaster.

The problem was the balance of risk for when Man went to the moon; Neil Armstrong showed with his heavy space suit, he could jump over buildings. This was akin to the cartoon character in the comics who wore a blue suit with a big S on his chest. The fact that gravity was approximately one sixth that of Earth so that if a child was brought up in such a gravity environment then on returning to Earth there would be quite the problem. Needless to say, the analogy for Mars was even worse so the whole trial was taken out of action. Now here was the need to have the data and knowledge from the past that would have been helpful but alas! There was none other than the knowledge from the past explorations that were in the computer banks of all the universities on earth.

Fallout from the big bang:

The universe was formed and space developed to hold the by-products of the tremendous explosions that emanated as it racked time, space and heralded the arrival of a small molecule or atom into existence and into action. The results of this action created planets, stars, hot suns that heat and cause chemical activities to undergo changes as observed in any *in vitro* laboratory on earth. But there are also suns that implode and add to the energy needed to be used in the further mixing of the cauldron that is the cosmos. As the cosmos exploded into existence there was need for space to hold the parts that were developing by quantum leaps. The imploding of an atom formed different systems of planetary stars, some primed to be homes for some life forms others just as storage depots of pure energy, elements and mineral resources.

About 5 billion years ago after the initial planet separations of the Big Bang took place; a small solar system was formed at the edge of which Mankind named the Milky Way. It was to be the home of carbon based life forms that became the forests, cold blooded animals and mammals which included the evolved species known as Man. The center of this universe was the sun, which garnered into orbit several planets and by the sheer force of its gravitational pull, due to its gigantic mass, forced them to remain as constant companions within its territory in set defined orbits. The sun was not just another star for it became the resource of energy and all that the living planet Earth needed to become the Garden of Eden. On this planet the conditions allowed stardust in the form of genetic material, from the Big Bang to metamorphosize into a myriad of different life forms, animal, plants microscopic, macroscopic and microbes. The question for all the thinkers on Earth to ponder is why on this planet and why should this unusual phenomenon in such an angry cosmos allow this relatively peaceful environment to develop and evolve?

This is the twenty-first century and little planet Earth is facing another phase in its cycle of birth and rebirth similar to what has been going on in the greater cosmos. However, the life form known as Man has become concerned that his activity may have caused an imbalance in the physical elements. From the human perspective, the cosmos really cares little for any carbon based life form over any other types. However, if there is a God that is kind then that God cares for Man. Man's activity includes the use of mineral wealth in the earth but he has over used its natural forests which maintain the atmosphere that supports Man, other animals and plant life forms. He has overused his food sources from land and the magnificent oceans, streams and rivers. His use of the carbon byproducts used to fuel all of his activities especially of locomotion had the downside effect of causing an earthly imbalance of the gaseous mix in the atmosphere.

Atmospheric imbalance:
The fallout of such an imbalance is that the atmosphere which has remained fairly constant for millennia has now begun to trap heat. This increase in heat has started to theoretically thaw out the frozen north and south poles of the planet. This could just be a cyclical event but there is concern that this heating of the surface of planet earth has to stop. If the frozen poles do indeed thaw out completely then the natural flow of hot water in the oceans, from the tropics to the northern cold waters will cease. If that was to occur then the seas will fail to be stirred up with dissolved minerals and oxygen. The projection is that biological life forms which are mainly microscopic will die off. The stew of the ocean's soluble chemicals will no longer be mixed by the natural flow of hot or warm waters into the cold arctic regions. This combination of hot and cold water currents is essential for the exchange of nutrients through these great north and south's current flows or tides.

Is this arrogance when one looks at the picture of the greater Cosmos? Man's attempt to come to terms with improving his conditions on which he has thrived for a few thousands of years is trivial but it keeps him mentally active. Such activity is necessary for his continued survival as his next evolutionary task is to go into space one day and learn more through exploration. In doing so, he would surely have taken advantage of the promise and the biblical promise of *dominion over the heavens and of earth and all therein*. It is within the realm of possibility, for he will try to set up populations in different planetary environments so that future offspring may change and adapt to the varying environments of the cosmos. This is probably the heaven that religions have preached according Man control over everything in the universe. The future of this carbon living form of life is a bright one as mankind's brain continues to develop, his restless mind and imagination will continue to probe. In doing so, he may grasp the bigger picture and that will be his tutoring as he explores the Cosmos.

Man's galaxy & his solar system:

In this planetary system with Earth, there is Venus, Mars, Saturn, Mercury, Jupiter, Neptune, Uranus and the smaller dwarf planets all circulating around the sun. Many of the larger planets have smaller bodies or moons that circle them. It has been found that these smaller bodies do have an impact on their larger companion, in keeping their internal heat under a constancy or control. On Earth, the moon affects the large bodies of water by assisting in their movements in the form of ebbs and flows. The limitation of Man's ability to travel into the outer reaches of space is currently hampered by limitations of technology and knowledge of the newer but dangerous forces in the greater cosmos. He is also limited by food resources, materials such as metals and fuel necessary to explore outside his own planet. However, probably his greatest short coming is his limited life span. This short life span is and will be his biggest hurdle for travel within his own sphere of existence, which is essentially his own solar system but he has time and generations to experiment.

Man can overcome much of this latter difficulty developing newer fuels that will last for his own life span. He has begun to use the powerful gravity of other planetary bodies in outer space to increase the speed necessary to propel his vessels or space droids into the darker regions of space. He is trying or experimenting, evolving and that indomitable spirit born from the dissatisfaction of the cosmos will give him the perseverance to continue until he solves the different problems in his pathway. Every problem solved will increase his capacity to thrive and with experimentation he will find the ways that will allow his survival in different environments and against different obstacles.

Choices:

Man will however be forced into making these decisions more quickly than he expects. He has been noting what has been happening in deep space for centuries. The carbon based fuels will soon be used up as will the natural gases for they will change into different gaseous forms that are useless at this time. He will continue to shoot man made products into outer space and once that is done there will no longer be any such products remaining on planet Earth. The cosmos has a ready and unlimited supply of radioactive fuel that is obtainable so the need for fuels will be solved in a matter of time. The risk will be greater than anything Man has faced on the earth during his evolution.

Will this stop mankind from his pathway that is needed for his development and indeed his survival as it appears to be foisted on him as a species? Is Man paying attention to the limitations of food resource, fuel and mineral stores of the earth? Where will the new products come from if Man is still earth bound? Man knows that he has first to curb his population growth to a level that allows sustainability of his species and his population. He is no different than any other animal population or plant species on earth and no different than the lemmings of old stories. If he uses up the food then he will have to limit his population so that the strong will survive.

A role for Divinity?

Will prayer help? Will the religious belief in the provisions by God, be the philosophy? How will this get rid of the futility facing mankind's survival in the midst of the shortages? Man will soon face these major problems in this the twenty first centuries. There is a small theory that was left to mankind in the early part of the twentieth century. It is known as the theory of *general relativity*. Whenever there is chaos, this theory steps in to bring balance and to some extent order. However, in the absence of resources it is possible that he may return to the brutal savagery of his early form. This is not a new biological fact for it is seen in other animal systems that primitive behaviour will develop in the absence of food, mates or limited territory.

THE COSMOS THROUGH THE EYES OF MATHEMATICIANS WITH COMPUTERS

This information is vital to the story, for Man has been fascinated by the stars and the universe from his beginning on this earth. Obviously, one should ask why this overwhelming obsession? When Man created God, he invariably looked towards the heavens or stars and imagined a figure up there that is listening and planning their future. The latter part may have some merit but surely there is not much chance that God is up there in the stars. If there is a God then perhaps he is around each and every individual or maybe he has his angels looking after his flock while he is remaking other parts of the cosmos.

The universe and the greater cosmos await man's entry and there will be great deal for man to learn through witnessing and experience. There is also much danger to man's fragile being and many will perish before moving ahead but for every life lost there will be understanding, growth and knowledge gained. Mans' species is prolific and will replace those lost numbers over a period of time. Only through research and experimentation in deep space will their lives not be lost in vain. Sacrifice is part of Man's being and he has survived many earthly catastrophes over his short life span. This is no different rather this is vital to the continued existence of Man as a carbon life form and surely the religions will support this as God's will? God will answer the prayers of Mankind in his own way.

EARTH'S REALITY:
Throughout the history of Man, earth's scientists and mathematicians have brought forth theories on the universe using the skill of mathematics. As have been described above, there may be some solace in the constancy of the planets seen in the skies above earth. The question is whether they really are in a permanent phase or a relatively constant position? If one supposed that they are not, then what are the consequences and have earth's scholars been looking after us with their research? The answer from the scholars is an unqualified "yes"

In Earth's solar system, the planets have been circulating around the sun as far as calculations go for approximately 4.5 billion years, give or take a million or so. In fact, one of my researchers corrected me by saying that it was 4.54 billion years. This constancy has been recorded from antiquity so one has only to accept that there is a measure of permanence. The problem is that man's lifespan is very short so the idea of permanence is limited to a human life time which is approximately70 to 90 years. The first observations confirmed what had been postulated through the history of man and that there were hundreds of extra solar planets as well as hundreds of nurseries or nebulae where planets were born. They all appeared to move in some form of gigantic orbit around a sun or some other greater neighboring planet. The force in fact was that of an untold gravitational force of which there is no one foci at this time of studying the cosmos. A study of the orbits of these exoplanets became the study of many mathematicians and this should be explained. Earth had done Trojan work on its study of space and its planetary bodies. Orbits did not just remain circular but many were oblong or elongated also referred to as eccentric. These planets took longer and shorter positions to their centre of power that appeared to keep them moving around in circles of varying sizes around a mass such as sun. The reason given for these elongated orbits was that there was essentially planetary chaos. The example cited was if one of the circulating neighbours were either kicked out of orbit or crashed into the closer planet or just imploded, the result would be temporary chaos. Whatever the reason there was *a gap* so to speak and the remaining planets just had bigger orbits to compensate.

To verify this explanation earth's astrophysicists used the example of the three planet Upsilon Andromedae system. It was estimated that the age of this system to be approximately 2.5 billion years. It was then theorized that there were four planets originally but the fourth one was ejected out of the system. The results of such a catastrophe of being kicked out of a system causes eccentric orbits to occur in the remaining other members of the system. However there is a fingerprint that shows what had happened and that is called the *signature of ejection* and that is what earth's scientists have measured and observed. Mathematically, it was estimated that it took approximately 8,000 years for the system to return to an eccentric configuration.

Gravity – understanding this is vital:

The whole system was postulated by Isaac Newton and thus brought the study of planetary orbits through his physics. He postulated that as *mass are attracted to a greater mass* depending on the distance of separation, all stems from the forces of gravity. His postulate then implied the order of orbits was held in balance by gravitational forces under a universal gravitational law. This theory could be used in his mathematical formula which could tell a planet's future pathway from its current location, its velocity taking into consideration the gravitational stresses or tugs in its pathway. When this analogy is used in earth's solar system our sun has control of 99.8% of the solar system mass. It then dictates where all the planets in our solar system should follow. However, observations have showed that all our planets do not keep a constant orbit but that these orbital changes can be ellipsoid at times. That has been attributed to Newton's theory of *gravitational pulls or tugs* exerted by the planets circulating our sun.

The gravitational tugs or pull forces *all add up* to be quite a force. Wherever there is a force then a counterforce often develops and that could have damaging effects on a planetary system. This was not a new phenomenon that was noted by Newton for it had been reported about three generations earlier by Mr. Kepler, who noted the "quirky paths" of some planets which he attributed to the *"simple, elliptical orbits in three dimensional space.* However, Newton and his workers had found and measured the trajectories of planets with enough precision to note that the orbits were not perfectly elliptical but changed from time to time.

Newton went on to study the planets Jupiter and Saturn but he found the mathematics insurmountable for his time and so felt defeated. This mathematical problem was solved in 1776 by Pierre Laplace. He showed that these tugs of gravity had a cumulative effect over a long period of time and the terms *commensurability/resonance = to the gravitational shifts or perturbations of two planets as they affect each other*. Apparently, these negligible little gravitational tugs if timed could produce a tangible long term effect. Laplace could then use his mathematical skills to look into the past of the planet's orbits and make predictions. He verified his postulate when he found a two thousand year old Babylon document that had the observations which he had predicted. He then predicted that *planetary orbits were inviolate and that the solar system was stable* and so his success was seen. He did not take into consideration that the cosmos had evolution of the planetary periods over many millions of years, which his mathematic formulae disallowed. So for his time, ego and confidence played its cruel joke for his work led to a postulate known as the *Laplacian determinism*. Essentially, if the *positions and velocities* of the planetary bodies were known, then the future could be predicted exactly.

This would be unraveled by other workers in the early nineteen century.

Resources of the Cosmos:
It would be a safe assumption to predict that planets or suns where these bodies have landed may have 'enrichment' in the form of an increase in minerals and energy but certainly an added mass. It is the continuing gift from the deep cosmos that replenishes stores of minerals, gases and maybe even molecular biological pieces of nucleic acids. The evidence is blatant on earth for it has the widest diversity of carbon based life forms that humans have discovered in his surroundings and continue to do so. The question asked is why this distribution from a human perspective is this 'enrichment' necessary and towards what end?

Unis must have been near to these hazards over its travels for over 5 billion years when it was still traveling. What a history it must have witnessed through space and time. Man did not exist as an evolved form in those early days. A parallel example on earth is that of our very old trees surviving several hundreds of years. Against the massive storms, temperature fluctuations, floods and mayhem that was earth, not even their rings of growth could tell the history of the physical conditions on earth during those years, to earth's botanists.

THE 21ST CENTURY USING ITS OWN MEASUREMENT OF TIME

What is there to say but writing in the year 2009, one billion seconds ago it was just the 1950's, the period when I, the author, grew up. One billion minutes ago, the birth of Christianity began with the prophet Jesus Christ. His mission survives today as does his clever interpretations of his time and missionary period has all been written and recorded for mankind. There appears to be a human need for explanations to understand their physical plight, so these remain as a source of comfort for hundreds of millions of people.

One billion hours ago mankind was not around indeed, the dinosaurs ruled this planet dominating all animal life forms. Only the majesty of the primal trees that thrived in the early days of the methane enriched atmosphere, were around to witness these giants. As earth evolved from a mixture of gases, caused by both the effects of its inner heat and the continuous eruptions of its volcanoes, the sun played its part in fuelling the magic of photosynthesis to take place. The moon allowed the water bodies to ebb and flow keeping the earthly chemical and biological stew turned over. These massive bodies of waters thus became enriched so that a myriad of life forms could find niches to thrive, survive and to reproduce their young in vast quantities and numbers.

The process of recycling water through evaporation to the gaseous state brought about rains that bathed the land. The sun found in the massive green trees the opportunity to make them the factories of gaseous absorption, while reprocessing and recycling the end products to ensure earth's creature metabolism and its own geologic changes remain evolving.

Earth- a living evolving entity:
Earth is a living vibrant and dynamic planet no less in its actions than the massive changes that take place in the greater cosmos. It has done so on a smaller scale imposing its will through its power to stabilize, warm, chill at night time; but causing the carbon cycle to take place through respiration in plant life. Two major climatic and botanical cycles evolved on earth that assists in maintaining its environment that allows carbon life forms to exist.

They are the carbon cycle and the photosynthesis cycles that take place on the surface of planet earth. While photosynthesis in plants allows them to use the energy of the sun's rays to bring about the combination of carbon dioxide and water to form carbohydrates or sugars in plants, the addition of nitrogen allows plant proteins to be formed. Nitrogen is added to plants either through adsorption from the atmosphere but the best studied manner of nitrogen introduction to plants is through the assimilation by bacterial forms living in nodules in the roots of plants.

Role of Microbes – the smallest life form in the Cosmos that is found on Earth:
These microscopic life forms take nitrogen from the air and form nitrates a soluble salt that is absorbed by plants. This process plays a role in the expanded growth of plants through protein build up. When plants are eaten by animals, animal proteins are formed. When plants and animals die then both carbon dioxide and water are released through the intercession of bacteria. However, this is not as straightforward as this simple explanation states for one of the smallest life forms in the universe, which is believed to be ubiquitous in the cosmos, known as microbes play a major role in these cycles. Without their presence the biological segment of this dynamic recycling of living matter would come to a standstill, at least on earth. These microscopic life forms are resistant and are very resilient. On earth many are found to be resistant to the extremes of temperatures, multiple of radiation types as well as, to many chemical poisons and anything that the cosmos can throw at it.

Microbes, in this instance, bacteria come in a variety of shapes and sizes with the important commonality that they are invariably microscopic. This statement will be addressed again dealing with the importance of size and its role in the cosmos. Needless to say, that in this instance one is dealing with a biological entity. Is a microbe alive was the question that is often put to the scientists and the answer is a qualified yes.

The physical description of a virus is that of a microscopic piece of RNA attached to a piece of protein forming a tail. The virus attaches itself to an animal cell by its proteinaceous tail. It then shoots its RNA into the cell, which goes directly to the source of enriched nucleic acids of DNA or the genetic centre or nucleus of an animal's cell. The virus RNA takes over the manufacturing activity of the animal cell and begins to reproduce its own particles. When the animal cell is full of viral particles, it ruptures and the millions of virus particles go to the next healthy cells and repeat the process. This is how a generic virus is known to multiply at this stage in time.

One explanation is that one can see bacteria, fungal elements and blood parasites under a light microscope but a virus can only be seen using an electron microscope. This explains the size differential. Fungi and bacteria are relatively easy to grow in the laboratory. Viruses are technically more difficult but they can be forced to replicate in living animal tissues.

Nature's composting agent:
Bacteria and fungi in nature break down dead animals and trees into their organic simple elements. These simple constituents are water, carbon dioxide and ash which are recycled back into the soil of earth. Carbon recycling is also done by bacteria taking a major role in the final disposition of dead carbon animal and plants. The gases released include methane, water vapour and carbon dioxide. There is also a nitrogen cycle but this depends on what is called "nitrogen fixing bacteria" which are usually found in the nodules of bean plants and other grasses.

When deciduous trees of the northern lands on Earth drop their leaves in the autumn, after building up the nutritive stores in their trunks and roots of new plant protein and sugars, they are broken down further by bacteria, fungi, simple grubs and worms in the soil. Their death and recycling is the same as that which occurs in the greater cosmos that continues to recycle energy in deep space. This renewal of all carbon based life forms keeps the energy in the system of this living planet in balance. Thus matter is neither created nor destroyed but recycled. One wonders whether this is the same principle that can be used when dealing with the massive actions of death and rebirth in the cosmos.

The examples of the recycling of elements, of energy sources and of rebuilding are all found on planet earth. As have been postulated before earth's *nurturing or learning academy* is here in this little oasis of cosmic calm that is earth.

Activity of Man:
The end of the 21st century has seen the almost total depletion of many of the earth's mineral deposits on land and there has been huge undertaking to mine under the great oceans. The oceans have very few of the original shoals of fish remaining especially since there have been failed international agreements to try and maintain whatever stocks of wild fish that may be remaining. A number of the outlying states still break the laws on ocean fishing that was agreed upon by the International Oceanic Protection Agency. Occasionally, the odd country allows poachers to fish for the very deep creatures of the oceans. If caught the odd fisherman may get away with a fine not confinement but tight laws allow for little chance of escape. Even when the total elimination of a species that maybe on the extinction those with money and power will break the law.

Preparing for outer space in the 22nd century:
Earth depended on some mining done in the early days of the mid 21st century, on the moon and on Mars but the different countries of Earth almost invariably, squabbled about their rights to a share of these last deposits from the nearby planetary bodies. The need to go further into deep space was coming to the crisis stage but very few of the world's countries had invested in the research done for almost a hundred years by the USA and European countries. Even when most of the research and education invested had been shared generously by these countries, with such great insight, there was a feeling of unfairness. This was felt much more so by the other great states such as China, the Federation of

Africa, South America Federation, with India and Pakistan leading the south East Asian countries that demanded more mining rights.

There was often the suspicion that they were not being dealt with fairly. The world council dealing with Disposal of Cosmic Element Discovery had little teeth in its legislations. Greed then as it was in the 21st century, still played a part by those richer countries always hoping to find that unusual and priceless mineral commodity.

Attempts by the lesser developed countries to bring down their population sizes had taken many years just to stabilize themselves. Indeed, were they not thrust into a state of near starvation and famine; they would not have taken the draconian steps to bring down earth's human population? Advances in medicine have allowed humans to live past 100 years of age easily. This has been both a blessing and a curse for the intellectual property of the world have increased with measurably benefit from the older population but it takes more energy and wealth to maintain these older scientists and statesmen. Their input was the bringing about of some stability in earth's family of countries through a patient diplomacy.

The other strange benefit of the shortage of elements from earth's depths and geology has allowed for more creativity in recycling and renewal into a range of new products. The early shortage of energy had been solved through direct use of energy from the sun. There have been many mechanisms that have allowed earth to tap into this continual nuclear power. However, space on land used to grow food to feed earth's burgeoning population, have been completely utilized. Man was forced to give up the eating of animal flesh and to make the most of plants as his sole source of food. There was little starvation on Earth, at this stage in time, for that was one resource that was truly shared with all countries. The other asset to Earth's limited resources was the renewal of the fight by mankind to continue research into outer space and to make the more difficult decisions that would govern the whole future of mankind.

SOCIAL REFORM:

It appears that the old world ageing politicians that held world stature and power were becoming weak and bureaucratic. The politicians began to waffle in making decisions and the role of ethics dominated so many decisions and this brought much progress to a stand-still. The whole process began to slow down and there was a long period of no progress. The lack of so many resources was shown to bring humanity on this little planet to a static level, if earthmen did not go out to the loaded store rooms that were located in deep space. Meanwhile as the cosmos expanded there were visible signs that the so called nearer planets were distancing themselves from earth. The *bullet had to be bitten* and this came from the new demanding youth with more open minded peoples of the have not countries. They have had to deal with so few resources for many years, that they became angry and knew that they had to take over power to make the hard decisions. When these new people came into the United Nations to make their pleas for advancement they had to be heard for they literally shouted down the old tired politicians and scientists that formed the senate of all house committees.

It was only a matter of time, before the new young politicians threw out the old and passive and replaced them with more dynamic groups of focused individuals that did not allow for any hindrances in their pathway and that included ethics. The world population of mankind had little choice for there had to be no more delays in opening up space exploration. This was done with the full knowledge that there will be loss of many lives but the alternative was just to dwindle away in frustration and in hopelessness. This was the state of life on earth for mankind at the end of the 21century. A new century was beginning and it became mandatory that humans of earth had to move out into deep space. The planning had began in earnest and the stars were continually looked at through the different earth monitoring devices as well as, the few left on the moon and on Mars by resident earth colonies.

The results from the many probes sent into space whose data had been evaluated and reviewed were now re-analyzed. The results showed newer decisions were been made on different interpretations of this older data collected over a hundred years past. This was going on and the excitement became infectious to the rest of earth's human populations. There was a new feeling of hope and adventure which opened up and was allowing many of the youth to enroll into the now diverse space programs. The specialties in science, engineering and in maintenance of the space vehicles that were needed to exist and to make this a success allowed for many recruitment centres to be filled. A massive retraining of the human work force began in earnest. In the midst of this hope, the astro-physicists became regular reporters on what was seen and what was occurring in outer space.

It was during this period that the impending catastrophe was uncovered and as this was a new period of enlightenment, it was announced immediately by those empowered to view the open cosmos. They reported that there appeared to be a huge comet traveling across the Milky Way and was heading into Earth's solar system. Earth's monitoring systems in outer space could just show the movement of a microscopic speck of light moving in an almost unfocused direction. Its size and composition were not possible at the first sighting even as it appeared to be coming closer to earth's solar system. The population of planet earth was both enthralled because of the heightened enlightenment while a small part had a dread of what might happen. The pundits were waiting their turn on the sidelines for just such an occurrence so that even more debate might take place and there was a high risk of paralysis again taking over running the world councils of aeronautical exploration.

OBSTACLES?

Religious bodies began their preaching on the need for repentance by the sinful majority. The news makers of both print, television and computer images began their delight in reporting all the possibilities of destruction under the disguise of in depth analysis. A large number of the intellectual groups had sincere discussions on the probability and risk of entering earth's solar system. The knowledgeable individuals who had a better than average opinion of what was taking place discussed their thoughts in camera. The enlarging body began to shine like a mini night time star. It now held the attention of the world's population. There were enough technology in circulation both owned privately as well as, by universities astronomy faculties, which opened up there technology to the surrounding public. On the spot basic knowledge was dispersed by graduate students in astronomy who came into their own as the senior faculty met in close quarters to discuss the possibilities.

The Astro scientists' analysis of Unis:

Many claimed that this small body appears to be no larger than the moon that is currently circulating earth as it has done for millennia.

26

It does not seem to have any vegetation on its surface but there were a few pock marked sites which must have been as a result of asteroid hits as it journeyed through the Milky Way. Its speed appears to be around the equivalence of one hundred thousand miles per hour. Its trajectory appears to be our sun. However, if it misses the gravitational pull of the sun then it will head straight on a collision course with earth.

Spectra analysis of the body shows it to be packed full with a mixture of approximately 94 elements once found on earth plus others that were indefinable. There also appears to be a frozen layer of water in the form of packed ice but it was difficult to know whether it went deep within the body. This was an unsure finding and could only be verified with a direct probe into its crust, an unlikely proposition at this stage. This unwelcomed visiting celestial body appears to be solid. There was a thought that this might have been a space type machine that would bring aliens into our galaxy. The implication being that it was hollow and that would account for its focused directional course that was becoming more certain daily.

The observation of other celestial bodies was given up by earth's scientists. Their collected focus was on this body, which boded doom for all living things on earth. This had happened once before during the Jurassic period on earth when all the dinosaurs were destroyed by a meteor hitting earth somewhere in the Gulf of Mexico. But that was small compared with this monster that was within sight of many human beings who could see it reflecting the light of our sun off its surface. The continual comparison by the archaeologists with events of the past for they postulated what was about to happen with little variation between members of this group. This disagreement between them and other specialists in space was a public and bitter one which was not very helpful to the people of earth who kept watching this celestial body making headway to earth.

The chance that earth would be missed was acute irrational optimism and there was no need but to prepare for total obliteration. This was extreme pessimism, none of which assisted the public universally as to what they should do or what would truly happen. Fratricide and matricide were occurring in the less evolved societies. The explanation from the civil rights bodies suggested that there was no need for the old folks to come to such a cosmic end. It was better for them to die, with all that they knew for most of their lives surrounding them. The rational appeared dim to those relatively less emotionally inclined but it was pragmatic. The ethical professionals had a field day on the television and communication networks. Whole retirement homes were under siege by the fanatics, who felt that it was the right thing to do, which was to end their folks suffering. When the argument came up that just maybe, they could survive and the young perish. The counter argument was they should not want the old to survive for they would be unable to do anything for themselves. They would be helpless and no good to the remaining survivors and would eventually die from some more tedious cause. There must have been a bit of selfishness also for then there would be more food for the young if the old were to be taken away. The irrational thinking was causing havoc, for the new leaders of earth just wanted to be efficient in all that they do. The coming disaster 'could also be organized' so that there would be a clean ending for mankind. This was a strange response to the deadly prospect that was the human being greatest nightmare.

There was a saying that may seem trite and dated but states *that God would destroy he first makes mad.* It has been the province of the ruling democratic governments for the past two centuries that wealth collected through taxes could be better used to spread benefit for all workers in the society. However, this benefit extended to building militia, developing new defenses, providing good water, public health and education for the masses. Many governments combined their wealth towards the universal good of all populations on earth. There was now a perceived threat from the cosmos and much of the public were no longer unintelligent. Even greater technology was extended to the military devices so much so, that if any of these weapons were used on earth, the planet would cease to exist. This was all undertaken to ensure the safety of earth's populations of peoples. These misguided principles all found their way into a book of policies. Then each policy becomes responsible for each government's program. After two hundred years of this bureaucracy build up, the endless list of policies and programs by successive governments combined to bring about a state of paralysis and inertia. The buildup of tiers of governments combines to demand more subsidies leading to more haphazard government interference. The point is this madness has gripped the populations of the world for there was terror of annihilation that has been speculated about, at least for two hundred years earlier.

The offer by the military to use their big technological armaments to destroy this advancing planet had been delayed because of bureaucratic discussions. This new mini planet was advancing rapidly. There needed to be an opinion for action to be undertaken as this was the last opportunity; for the small adventurer was too close. If shattered then there would be a rainfall of smaller asteroids that would surely guarantee the destruction of earth in a more cruel form than by just a direct hit. This singular suggestion had lost its promise because there was no policy recommending action. The new government had lost its power to make a decision now it was too late.

NASA Scientists:
The only sobering suggestions, in the midst of this dilemma, were from the group of scientific workers at the American space agency, NASA. Specifically, those associated in observing the advance of this round object coming towards them from outer space. Their instruments continue to measure every iota of the phenomenon in great detail and all the information was recorded and filed in buried electronic data storage repository deep underground. They had done what they could with their families many of whom were closed in underground on their campuses. They used this time to picnic, to play with their young children and to make as though all was normal. The smaller children felt that they were in a holiday camp with their mums and dads. The lines on the faces of the women, who were the mothers, sisters and older siblings, showed as deep cracks on their tired faces. The men just continued to work even more intensely.

There was continual contact with the European agency, the World Space Agency just co ordinate all the research from the Chinese, The Indian, The South American and the Israeli led Middle East group of scientists. Data poured in from all these agencies many with concrete findings but lots of hypotheses were being suggested. As with all statistics the collection of data will include a number of absolutely nonsensical suggestions. This massive collection of data all flowed into the underground storage centres where the warehouse of all earth's space activities was contained.

One such suggestion was that earth should send a loaded spacecraft of nuclear bombs directly into the pathway of this monster of doom and crash it, into its surface. The problem was that earth's nations had long ago destroyed these weapons and none were to be found on earth. It would have taken the scientists much too long to recreate these nuclear weapons of the early 21st century. It was thought that the Russians or the Chinese may have still have had a few stored out of sight of the international monitoring safety treaty organization. In fact, these countries did live up to the extent of the treaty and there appeared to be no trickery or deceit of this trust.

Unis was moving along quite smartly in a focused direction towards entering Earth's solar system. The scientists' cameras were focused as it made a loop and came into an orbit close to Pluto. Then to everyone's surprise it made another maneuver and entered in an orbit with Neptune, then moved to that of Uranus. This jumping from one orbit to another was a real cosmic phenomenon that many thought would eventually have a disastrous ending for the creatures of earth. Some thought that it would just leap into our sun and be destroyed. Then *Unis* came into the orbit with Mars after skipping through Saturn's orbit then to Jupiter. Each loop brought hope that it would be pulled in by these larger planets. All that the people of earth saw daily and now constantly was that it was shining larger and brighter in the sky. This was reported by all earth populations who bore witness from their geographic position. It shone no longer as a grey body but almost like the full moon of earth.

The astrophysicists quietly worked out that the reason for this "jumping phenomenon" was due to the continuous force of the suns' gravitational power. This was further explained as more force on a moving *Unis,* was understandable as it got closer to the sun. Apparently, it would be more difficult to move a moon that was already stationed around a planet for it was a stable entity and would take too much gravitational energy from our sun.

Unis' Last Leap into Orbit

It has been known for years that the earth's moon was slowly moving away from its centuries' old position while remaining in orbit around earth. It was just a guessing game as to the reason for this departure. Many thought that some time in the cosmic clock, when it was necessary it would just adjust itself back to where it was when the earth, sun and moon came into being some ten billion years earlier. The phenomenon was not worth studying but was just noted for it had no direct impact on earth or its population of mankind.

The moon did indeed have an effect on earth's oceans and especially on the nocturnal small animals. This author has seen the moon rays shine as a bright focus of light on the surface of the deep oceans and noted the arrival of very large sea birds sitting in its glow. It was also noted that many large shiny sea bodies, thought at the time to be dolphins, came into its light but appeared only to play. These dolphins appeared, for some unknown reason, whenever there was a full moon and its beam of light struck the surface of the deep oceans. Others have reported that many of the large cetaceans would behave in a similar manner. The depletion of the food source was the cause of the demise of these majestic creatures. They now remain as just a memory to a few, who felt themselves very lucky to have seen them in the wild and not just in manmade ponds.

La Luna has been eulogized as the reason for a great deal of mankind's emotional and romantic behaviour. It was thought, in a more primitive time during the evolution of man, to be the reason that men became Mad. In earth's literature, it was a time when the mythological creatures such as werewolves came to bay at the sight of the moon. Men who were bitten by a werewolf would change from the smooth skin human handsome beings, into this creature covered with hair, huge fangs and the head of a wolf when the moon was full. The moon did have a great impact on mankind as he evolved into the being that he is today.

When Man first walked on the surface of the moon all the school boy's theories of the lesser gravity were observed and later verified. The first earth men leapt about in their heavy space suits as though they were filled with helium. The lesser gravity did allow ordinary men to perform as Olympians. Years later, when man revisited the moon, they found some water in the form of frozen ice. A camp was built underground as protection from the crashing of asteroids. Communication systems were set up and there was a bold undertaking to try and mine some of its mineral wealth. This was OK to begin with, but the cost of bringing back ore samples proved that it was not worth the effort. If there was a source of energy on the moon, which would allow Man to refine the ore or even allow for the building of space ships or manufactured products, then it could be a proposition worthy of the investment.

After attempts by the Americans, the European space agency tried but they all came to the same conclusions. The Japanese tried and they were followed by the Chinese, then the Indians but they all came to similar difficulties and eventually to similar conclusions. It was a good place to set up telescopes to view deep space while sending back signals to earth. Mining was abandoned on our next celestial body, the companion of earth for many hundreds of years.

Unis was in the same orbit of Mars and it appeared to be stabilizing in this orbit for it had not moved for more than a month. However, from one of NASA's viewing telescope mountain sites, it was recorded before each move to a new orbit, *Unis* would shudder for a few hours or more before making the move to a new orbit.

Both the professional scientists as well as, an army of keen hobbyists were studying the movement of this new glowing body in the night sky. Once the information leaked out that it would move when a 'shudder' began every amateur got hold or made their own viewing instruments to try and guess when *Unis* would move again. From the data to date, the next orbit to move to would be that in which earth and its moon have been using for many billions of years.

UNIS' TURN:

The emotions of earth's population varied from wishful thinking that all will be well to a helpless "frozen in the head lights phenomenon" The population stared in disbelief at this new beautiful round silver object that would soon be the cause of their demise. Then after what would have been a considerable time but in fact was just an earth's month, there was a 'shudder' and *Unis* moved quickly into earth's orbit. It appeared to slow down but was visibly moving, slower and becoming larger as it got closer to earth. Earth's youth began to work on their hand held computers measuring the advance first by meters and feet to begin with; Unis moved slowly closer to the earth and the phenomenal size caused many to gasp at the silver spectacle. It appeared to hang under the tremendous force of the sun which was now restricting its movement.

The whole of surface of earth was lit up regardless of where anyone was on this planet. There were massive wind storms that seem to have developed from nowhere. The meteorologists were completely stymied and their instruments were totally unreliable. Slowly the communication satellites began to stop working. Maritime bodies reported on the massive buildup of waves rushing towards shore lines on planet earth. It appeared that every ocean became stirred up by the pull of this new celestial presence. Physical forces brought earth populations into panic and much energy was now focused on survival in hitherto safe cities. Because of the risk of a global warming back in the early twentieth century earth populations began to move away from the prime seashore locations.

Further along in this time, flash floods and tsunamis developed and caused more cities to move away with its populations onto the higher ground and to the interior lands of earth's surface. A few underground cities in the oceans were attempted but the number of undersea earthquakes soon put an end to that experiment even though a small fringe group continued to live and to farm the depths of the oceans. But the surface lands of earth were almost completely developed for agriculture and for living space. True, buildings were built upwards to massive heights but the supporting systems necessary to keep such populations employed and entertained took much valuable land space.

UNLEASHED TERROR

The clouds increased many hundred folds and there was a twilight darkness that embraced earth with the presence of *Unis*. As the clouds built up from over 3 billion tons of water in the atmosphere to almost double that amount, the shady darkness brought an even more sinister atmosphere. The rain was falling all over the surface of the earth and it was continuous and unrelenting. Massive lightening storms were continuous and became the norm. The news media, using outdated communication lines reported with unusual glee details of floods and of tsunamis that were pounding away at the earth's surfaces. The erosion of huge rocky surfaces such as the Cambrian shield off the coast of North America dropped into the Atlantic Ocean. This was reported and it fed the public with details of the damage that was very significant.

The earth began to experience a loss of sunshine because of the blocking of the sun by the massive cloud cover of water. Nocturnal animals appeared to be the best adapted to this change in weather. However, the depression of human beings in the total absence of sunshine began to rise and this brought about its own problems. The offshoot was the deviant behaviour in humans, many behaved like caged animals. This was cause of much human misery on a scale never witnessed before in the history of mankind. It seemed to be months on end with the semi darkness covering the earth and indeed time appeared to move quickly.

There was the feeling that an ice age was about to take over the planet as the tropics began to cool down. The temperature dropped further in the northern countries and the news of *Unis* deteriorated into just news. Earthlings had to cope with the catastrophes occurring daily on earth, in their towns, cities and environment. People began to pay more attention to their immediate plight than pay attention to the different news media, which were finding more difficulty with staying on the air. Yes, *Unis* was still being observed by a smaller group as the fear of massive deaths in different countries began to be recorded and the shouts for assistance took the ruling world councils time for they sent out the marine core of engineers to take over the control and to provide assistance. The health and safety army took off next in answer to the call for attention. They were left in control to give support and to use whatever they needed but preference was to be given to those that were salvageable. In the midst of all the surface chaos, the strange observation happened. There appeared to be two moons every day and evening. While one was waning the other was rising and this while magical, began to play on people's nerves and after several weeks of this darkness and chilly temperatures, there was an apparent change in the wind patterns.

The weather began to stabilize but the temperatures continued to become colder across all the time zones of earth. It was reported by the outlying scientist group that were stationed at the poles, that there appeared was an increase in ice thickness. This was a phenomenon not witnessed for over a hundred years. As new ice was forming in massive amounts at both poles on earth, the snow falls increased to massive proportions not seen for a century or more. The chaos and hardships overwhelmed the services but the robots designed to clear away snow and to build dykes were working overtime with some human assistance. Indeed, it was also reported that the highest mountain peaks in the Himalayas, the Urals, the Rockies and Andes all began to build up massive peaks of ice but in larger and heavier amounts than had ever been recorded for many years.

It appeared that as the earth cooled, water from the heavy clouds began to freeze and to rebuild up the mountain peaks similar to that of a hundred plus years earlier. Similarly it was reported after about six months that the poles were expanding and so the world populations began to prepare for the global ice age. While the environmentalists were having a hay day with these supposedly reformations of the earth identified as an occurrences from the past, there was a universal winterlike weather. In the meantime amidst this cooling the winds maintained their strength and after about three months there was a semblance of order but under a different more hostile environment. The oceans were being fed with much biological material from land. In opposition, the massive volcanoes awoke as a chain erupting at all the old sites streaming into the oceans causing more land mass to be formed. The biologists made a startling observation which was the return of bird-songs to the towers of the big city complexes. This simple announcement seemed to quiet many a population. The despair was unbelievable for many of earth's populations had been destroyed as the cruel waters on earth continued to wreak havoc.

Consequently, the heavy dark clouds that had been formed when *Unis* came into an orbit with Earth persisted for well over 6 months. After about the 9 months there was visible thinning of these dark clouds into a lighter pale grey to white covering over Earth. But the rains and severe wind storms continued but many a population were becoming accustomed to their constancy. The system of water disposal through the sewer control engineered operating was overwhelmed and old fashioned flooding took place. This was disastrous for those still living near rivers, lakes and on flat terrains. Food crops were washed away and many animals were destroyed.

EARTH'S ALLY: THE MOON A FORCE UNTO ITSELF

As the population of Earth watched the new blazing full moon, they soon began to lose interest on their impending doom and stared in wonder at this new celestial beauty which shone both day and night. The world body dealing with the oceanographic monitoring began to see even more massive tsunamis that would begin destruction as soon as *Unis* came closer to earth. Their projections also indicated that with the force of the two moons there would be a cosmic tug of war and the earth would split into two parts. There were projections of hurricanes that would never cease as a number of *Voodoo* scientists took over the world media. The religious groups had to dig up Noah as proof that God was at work. Strange that God was again using the old system to destroy the sinful Man that he had created in his own image.

The population was again placed into a state of panic. However, this time they knew that it would not be just a catastrophic smashing into the earth so that all life as Man has known it would cease but more pragmatically it would be complete obliteration instantly. Now they did not have to fear that the destruction would be a slow death as the powerful forces of gravity now in play between the earth, the sun and the two bodies would just cause terrestrial havoc. God was at work says the religious leaders and Armageddon would soon be at hand for the wicked and the world of man will disappear. This was all foretold in the bible teachings of the New Testament but the faithless paid little heed to the warnings of God.

As *Unis* came closer, the tides of the massive oceans changed their routine and moved in the opposite directions, It was the same as watching water going down the sink in Australia. In fact, this reversal allowed the oceanic tides to move in the opposite direction of the northern hemispheres and the surrounding countries. The winds changed and the flow of the jet stream began to lag and to move into deeper curves so that the weather began to change in extremes in the now tropical countries as well as those in the temperate climates. This all began to occur in twenty four hour cycles. In short, if the weather was indeed unpredictable, even when earth had advanced to the extent of having a bit of control over changes in humidity and generally of the weather, it was totally uncontrollable with the arrival of *Unis*. Instruments monitoring the weather were now useless.

The news of the world was interrupted for the satellites were now non functional. The local news making operations showed old fashion flooding and mudslides reminiscent of the early part of 2000 or earlier over 200 years ago. However many people did not see these news items for they were too busy trying to keep alive. The catastrophes caused by hurricanes, increased storms were daily occurrences and the world army that was formed to deal with any global catastrophes was stretched to the limit of being ineffective. None the less, they persevered and continued to work alongside local populations, robots and the built in protection barriers that were developed many decades earlier. The deaths of whole cities and even countries mounted with each report from the army to the governing bodies.

If ever there was a shock to the sensibilities of the world complacent leaders, here it was in full force. Nature came back with a force to shake up mankind and to remind him in no uncertain way that he was just one species and a very fragile but greedy one at that. This played into the hands of the different religious groups for here was retribution from God Almighty. It was the Fall of Rome all over again but this time it was the end of the world. As communications began to be interrupted many folks just got to hear what their neighbors said and in some way this was a true village of the 20th century mentality that was happening. The small groups of inhabitants in the very tall buildings went down to lower floors as the buildings swayed under the stress of the massive wind storms that persevered for long periods of time. The people could see the new visitor that spelled doom for mankind but it appeared as a silver dish reflecting the bright night time light of the sun. The earth's own moon seemed smaller and less bright to many but the apparition of this terror in the skies did not allow many to sleep or rest.

REFLECTION:

However, as is the nature of the human being, a few societies and many of the educated groups paused to observe, to think and from their relative safe domiciles built into the heights of mountains or deep within caves on high ground, began to contemplate the new phenomenon with wonder and without fear. This was a sight to enjoy for there were now two moons circulating earth. Both glowed with silver light reflected from our sun and both had the familiar grey shadows denoting indentations or some other optical geological artifacts or impacts by meteorites on the surface.

The most frightening aspect was that now there were regular occurrences of eclipses of the sun, then of the moons. The new body remained stationary for a period of six months then the period of time extended to one year. The population of Earth had settled down amid the controls and world support for the disasters of climate changes taking place, were being tackled. The international news stations went back to the neglected line cables and somehow opened up their communications. Among these communiqués included the weather channels, which had a firm fixed feature in their daily and nightly reports. It all dealt with the position and presence of *Unis*. The effect and the impact on human behaviour all were attributed to this visitor from the deep cosmos. The talking heads dominated the headlines again, which now incorporated professionals such as astro physicists, meteorologists and the arrogant futurists, none of whom had any practical experience of what was taking place with this new moon. The lack of substantial solutions was quite obvious to the remaining of earth's populations. All suggestions that were put forward were untried hypotheses none of which stood up to a time of this phenomenon and so there were limitations of human thought by all the so called specialists. The debates discussions continued on close circuits to the few that were suffering any communication interruptions.

False feelings of security:
A feeling of lackluster confidence began to crawl back into normal life for the majority of educated peoples. There was a circle of people that lived in quiet fear and a silent majority that had apprehensions of this new visitor which was now viewed as the fabled *Sword of Damocles*. There was a need for balance of thought and understanding. Neither the religious few that preached the philosophy of fate and the need for redemption nor the pessimists that destruction was certainty, did anything to bring about an understanding. Earthlings just waited for the big bang when Earth would be smashed into stardust. There were the optimistic politicians who in fact brought about some solace by explaining that if *Unis* was to stay then mankind would have no option but to visit it. In fact, there was a quiet belief that without any evidence, all were in good hands. Neither group was giving obvious hope to the societies of the world, but ordinary people wanted some optimism.

In the meantime, NASA scientists along with its allies around the world were taking a more cerebral approach but were never available to make any public statements. The few began to see a stabilizing effect of the two moons. There was no one factor in their calculations and readings of their sophisticated instruments that would give the conclusive evidence. Larger orbiting Earth satellites failed to work and they were needed to make some definitive conclusions but all results failed to materialize. Their calculations of the gravitational forces of the sun based on its mass and the fact that it stabilized the orbits of the planets along with the new gravitational impact of *Unis* continually gave the end result. *Unis* was not finished with moving from this orbit. Earth's gravitational pull was in fact bringing its own gravitational force in favour of a crash onto its surface.

The matrix of algebraic calculations of distance, speed, time and the gravitational forces also revealed that *Unis* was still creeping microscopically slowly towards Earth. This was the cause for concern with this small group of scientists, who were also keeping in touch with the European, the Indian and Chinese fellow scientists who also verified these findings. Then almost into the twelfth month, observers of *Unis* saw the now familiar shudder occurring at night time in the northern countries. Then *Unis* began to visibly move towards Earth appearing larger in size. The atmosphere looked more like a convex mirror. The oceans appeared to leap towards the heavens. The reflection of the sun became too bright for human eyes.

The crash was about to happen and the global connections of satellites and other microwave communications all fell silent. In this silence, the cries and fears of the human populations were frozen as though there was an ear plug into the ears of all who watched in awe as the globe overhead began to become larger by the seconds. The wrath of God was at hand and he wanted the sinful population of this planet to know his anger. But God is also a merciful God and he did in fact create Man in his own image. He also created the theory of *general relativity*. Crouching in fear was the position of all those who stared into the heavens for that was the fixture that every human being were caught up in, except for the few who could not move to the outside and depended on the televised visions. The churches also hid many who came begging for a last minute reprieve.

As obliteration was about to happen, the NASA scientists calculation worked out to the exact minute when the closeness will be unavoidable and could not recede but have impact with Earth. It was like playing with the gun with one bullet a game of a cruel form of Russian roulette. As *Unis* slowly approached held from a catastrophic impact by very strong gravitational forces, the impact of Earth's gravity still weighed in favour of a quick crash. Others worked out that before the impact and the slowness of *Unis* movement, most of the organic life forms on the surface of the earth would just be terminated before impact.

The voices of the human population and the sound of Earth's natural forces, such as volcanoes, earthquakes all combined to make this planet shudder like a marble in an empty match box. Just as suddenly before the second of impact, *Unis* pauses. It began to slowly shudder.

However, instead of moving towards the Earth, it began to retreat very slowly. The religious leaders said that God was taking a stand and would let those faithful live or maybe the forgiving God had taught Man a lesson. There was silence from the governments as the obvious sight of a slight movement then a retreating *Unis* was seen by all of Earth's remaining populations.

There was a distanced radio wave connection from an outpost whose signal was focused on the NASA Scientist group. The connection was poor but it became stronger as the call was recognized as coming from the scientists located on one of the small observatory towers located in the Andes of South America. The message was focused and addressed to the NASA and European Space Groups. These scientists were shouting in excitement that NASA and the European Space scientists should turn away from *Unis* and focus their attention on Earth's moon. When they did they found that the companion of Earth for over 4 billion years was doing the "shuddering dance" not unlike *Unis*. It has been known that Earth's moon was moving away from earth in minuscule amounts for centuries. It was only in the early part of the 21st century, that this observation was calculated and verified by the world group of scientists.

As NASA and European scientists turned their collective attention to Earth's moon and companion, they saw that it was indeed shuddering not unlike the visitor *Unis*. There was a pause as the collective brains of the earth's astro scientists brought the two celestial figures into a combined focus. Their instruments began to become erratic and were useless for the tasks that they were designed to do. From the South American observatory a heavily accented English voice reported that they were working out the gravitational forces using a small handheld computer. They were convinced that the moon was closing in on Earth from the opposite side of *Unis*. The visitor was being restrained by the combined power of the gravitational forces of the sun and moon in neutralizing the Earth's gravitational force. *Unis* was stopped in its track.

Then, as it shuddered, *Unis* began to retreat to the original locum that it had occupied over the many months in orbit around Earth. The moon began to move closer to its original position which it had occupied for many millions of years previously. Earth's moon paused.

Unis remained still and the two Moons of Earth became a phenomenon. There was a balance of powerful gravities but the questions of why and how remained for there were no answers. However, reporters of the world began the doomsday scenario of when the Earth will be destroyed and every day that the population observed the new body in the sky, the reminder that the sword could drop at any time became tangible. Different theories were bandied about and the range of 'when' not 'if' the catastrophe would take place played out as a sort of enthusiastic horror story. Indeed, the doomsayers had their field day but the scientists remained silent just observing, measuring and recording voluminous data.

In all this chaos the few untouched populations of earth did little but ate drank and imbibed of all the pleasures that were around them. Many hate crimes were committed for the laws and robot forces were insufficient to police the world. The human sorrow could not be measured or contemplated for there was talk of deaths in millions of people mainly in the tropics while many died of cold and starvation. The population scanners showed massive cities drowning beneath hundred foot high waves. While whole Island populations in the huge Pacific Ocean were completely wiped out, the smaller islands of the southern regions could not be seen for they were completely submerged. The volcanoes of those islands became active and were spewing out mountain high lava as the earth regurgitated its guts for the mantle had been bridged.

The story was no different for the Islands of the Caribbean, throughout the Pacific and those in the Indian oceans. Many of the very wealthy had made their homes on these supposedly safe retreats of luxury. Catastrophe of the type that planet earth was facing had no respect for either power influence or position. The species of mankind was under attack by an alien from deep space. It came not in a space ship or in any romantic vehicle as the movie story tellers of old depicted but in a crude, cold but wondrous site. There were no ray guns or laser directed powerful arms doing the destruction only a silent presence of a lost moon from the deep cosmos standing quietly reflecting the light of the sun. This too was the power of a divinity for it was unbelievable to behold. It caught Man's imagination at a standstill.

Theories Abound:

As earthlings became accustomed to the sight of the two moons, the protective stations of control for the weather showed that flooding were enhanced; the work robots took on the heavy lifting and repairs. A strange complacency took place among the now smaller populations of Earth. This did not prevent the news media from continuing their reports of which much was just plain inventive and speculation. Their reports on mayhem just did not have the impact anymore on the public at large. The scientists were very cautious and only allowed a little of confirmed information to be let out. However, one theory that struck a note of a plausible scenario was expressed in an international news cast.

Essentially, while there may be a quiet period in the circulating moons around the Earth, the possibility of an even more catastrophic destruction was building up. This local scientific self appointed authority stated quite casually that this was really the calm before the storm. It explained that as the moon was adjusting to the strain of the gravitational pull of both the sun and earth, it was only a matter of time when it will lose the battle and rush towards earth from one side while *Unis* would come in from the other side of Earth. The explanation was that the orbits that each moon held were now being shared and were smaller. It was also postulated that the sun would eventually lose control of the orbits in favour of one over the other. Earth will be crushed like the boiled egg in a sandwich between two moons. The airwaves remained silent for about 24 hours as the grip of fear now raced anew across the world. There was a shuddering of both the moon and *Unis*, imagined by many who appeared hypnotized by the phenomenon of two moons circling earth. Several younger scientists began their calculations and tried to explain in scientific jargon what was actually happening, The use of observances by many from around the earth was used as data for these projections.

The populations of the Earth stared fixated and paralyzed staring involuntarily at the silver domes, which could be seen for 24 hours. This was a true attack by a cold invader from deep space and there was nothing that earthlings could do to protect themselves.

The story of Unis continues in the next novel.

PROTO – THE FIRST

INTRODUCTION

There may be some order in the great depth of space where humans may just have grown from the seed of a Mother Creation Tree located in the deep recesses of the Cosmos.

It all began when the earth ship was searching for new life forms and documenting stellar activities. The main ship seeded scientists in groups, whose task it was to visit the sites of interest, record their findings but should never interfere if there were other living life forms present. There were debriefings after every trip and all was recorded into the ship's massive computers and sent home to the collected pool of knowledge.

On one of these investigative voyages, three volunteer scientists were sent off to look at a solar system which was located approximately two weeks away from the mother ship. This was a slightly unusual solar phenomenon since the long range scans revealed that there was one sun with only one circulating planet, which appeared to have a lush carbon based flora.

The members chosen for this exploration were – Leslie Ram, Tara Luapog, and Len Denis. It was easy enough to see why these three were chosen since Leslie Ram was a qualified career space Microbiologist with speciality in minuscule life forms of the universe. Tara Luapog is a brilliant and sharp female engineer, whose specialty included the search for organic minerals, water as well as, to assist with the documentation and locations of these sites during exploration of deep space. She also knew it was vital to look for habitable planets, which was a necessity for the humans from earth. She was chosen also for her leadership skills. Len Denis was also well qualified in communications and piloting the craft but also duplicated some of Tara's skills in detecting and searching out minerals – the inorganic forms. It was not a typical crew which would cover all aspects of a true research mission but it had the basic ingredients for an away team, involved in scouting out an unknown planet.

It was not long before this small crew set off to check out the section of the quadrant which was been mapped by the parent ship. This was almost a routine mission. For the crew, it was a chance to get out of the routine daily chores and get excited of doing anything else. The small module was provisioned for a two week stay, which was the norm. And so it passed that the three man personnel found themselves communicating with each other. They were aware of each other but did not have the opportunity previously to officially meet or socialise with each other. It was common on the parent ships for the crew to acquaint themselves with personnel of similar interests and some go further by trying to check out the entire crew including the senior leadership team. This could be quite the task since at times the crew contingent could be as high as a thousand personnel. So with feelings of goodwill for each other as there were only the three of them for the next two weeks, Tara opened the orders on the small hand held computer which outlined their respective jobs. It was very much as described in their individual curriculum vitae. The only exception was that the two men had to obey the orders of the leader Tara Luapog. They settled into the routine of their shuttle and knew that they would be at their destination within 24 hours at their current light speed.

It was a very calming sound as they awoke to hear Tara say, "we are there, rise and shine lads." They looked at their screens and saw the sun, which was like all the others they had encountered around the many planets. The shuttle was equipped with sensors of all variety and types so it began the automatic process of logging information as to distance, radiation type present, making photos of almost everything in its path to a radius of almost a light year away. As the tons of information sped in front of their screens, they quickly adapted to the salient parts necessary to each of their respective portfolios. It was not long before they had visual contact. They had been on the research ship for over three years but it was always exciting when they went into a new area of the cosmos and saw planets for the first time. It was always the feeling of being first to see new territory and new frontiers in space.

In front of them was a sun which was being dated by the shuttle's computers, measuring its spectral composition, radiation types and all physical aspects many of which were pre programmed for others to evaluate. What was fascinating to them was the planet circulating around the sun once every twenty four hours. It was similar to that of earth and as they got nearer and slowed to begin observations, it looked like earth must have been before the presence of man. So far the scanners revealed a densely treed planet with no obvious large bodies of water but the atmospheric mixture of gases showed an earth-like combination of twenty percent oxygen, some hydrogen (1%) and nitrogen almost 70%. There was carbon dioxide and other inert gases taking up the remaining 19 %. Humidity was approximately 60% and there was some cloud formation, which were small and not long lasting. All this was good news for it was not necessary to wear the bulky and cumbersome space suits with portable breathing apparatus. Both Tara and Len double checked the entire portable instruments pack to make sure they were all functioning correctly. Les began the planning of his experiments focussing on looking at the microscopic life forms of both plant and animal varieties that may even be in the atmosphere. Biological scans tend to look at the large presence of carbon based forms so it was always risky when microbial forms are being investigated. Earthlings had to approach this task carefully for there might be infectious microbes that would love to find the inhabitant of a humanoid body in which to find safety and a niche, they may occupy. Study of the microbial flora could only be done after landing.

With their respective responsibilities outlined and after satisfactory answers to inquiries, the three crewmen were prepared and ready to land and have a look around. There were communicators and space scooters, which would cover great distances. It was up to Les to go out first and to check the air, radiation and of course the microbial world. Since it was necessary for everyone to be cross trained, his task was to verify what the others had already found out using the technology on the shuttle. Len took over the tasks of making sure all the hand held analysers, communication devices, the scooters were functioning properly and were linked directly into the shuttle computer system.

There was also a backup system which allowed information gathered by the shuttles continuous monitoring system to frequently download the accumulated information to the parent ship which was several light years away. With all the safety precautions and mechanical systems checked out, Les left the shuttle which Tara had landed in the middle of a clearing in the lush green forest. This was strange to find such a spot since it appeared that the total planet surface was covered with an almost impenetrable rain forest similar to that of the Amazon forests on planet earth – a long time ago. At least that was the picture which came immediately to their minds.

When Tara pointed out the clearing to them it was difficult for them to see it at first, since it was a small turf covered savannah. As the leader in charge, Tara made the decision to land and there were only silent murmurs of positive approval. It may be because there was an internal excitement of just wanting to land. This feeling appears to all workers who spend most of their lives on these long range exploration space ships. The mere site of any land in the form of planets, large silently gliding comets and old burnt out stars, were always a welcomed site and there was the anxiety of just wanting to feel a form of terra firma under one's feet.

Les quickly affirmed that the atmosphere was indeed acceptable to humans. The radiation was almost non-existent and all he could pick up on his micro monitor was bits of dust particles and some pollen. The information sent back to the two in the shuttle was verified by the larger backup system, which was placed on continual monitoring to the exclusion of only maintaining life support. A quick screen to check for toxicity of the pollen revealed a mild collection of nutritionally trace factors with no toxins to carbon based life. After the monitoring of the life support environment, Les raised his eyes for the first time to see himself, surrounded by some of the largest and healthiest trees he could have ever imagined. The grass felt lush and soft even through his mesh of plastic and metal covered feet. He was able to move so quickly in spite of his clothing and indeed he could feel the slight warmth of the sun through his space suit. It appeared as if his own space suit support system had shut down and as though he was free of artificial protective clothing. Towards this end he reported back that they had found another earth planet. The information forwarded back to him that it was alright to take the next step which was to try breathing in the planet's air. He shut down his own air supply and through a system of filters fresh air passed into his lungs and he felt a purity and ease in breathing, as his lungs filled with the natural air, which felt fresh and wholesome. He turned it off and returned to his own air supply system. It was almost like a jolt for it appeared that he was re breathing a stale source of air which he was. His body returned to the response of the artificial but he felt a longing to open up to the atmosphere again but he waited for the return of the approval system checks from Tara and Len on the shuttle.

It seems like ages before they responded when in actual fact it was just five or more minutes before he had approval to remove his head gear breathe regularly for another 30 minutes but he was to return his head gear at any sign that was alien to him. He was free to move closer to the woods while remaining in sight of the crew. As he got closer to the trees, there were small flowers on the turf but one had to focus down without the head gear. His eyes remained sharp and he also found a freedom of movement brought on by the fact that his head could move around freely while his eyes scanned everything around him.

Maintaining eyes on his hand held monitors, he bent down to feel the grass with his bare hands and there was a softness, which almost caressed his skin. He just thought that this is to be expected since he had only been in contact with space equipment for the past fifteen years of his training. The trees and food plants on the parent ship were only handled by the space gardeners and no one else was allowed to go into the garden. It was considered a security area since it was responsible for over 80 percent of their life support system providing food, oxygen and moisture to the whole vessel. Here he was feeling all this vegetation around him with no competition from fellow humans. He also understood that he was also playing the guinea pig for the others on the shuttle, who were monitoring even his psychological responses. There was a levity which he had to respond to but this was easy because of his scientific training. Failure to respond from the tried and proven policies of space flight could get one into a great deal of trouble, not only for the individual but for his colleagues. Indeed, it may jeopardise the whole mission, which was extremely costly. He had attended enough mission debriefings to see the effects of those individuals on sour missions. Non-the-less, this freedom he was feeling became an urge to strip off his space suit and to run around and shout but he resisted all these primal feelings and forced himself to go through the steps outlined in the protocol. He replaced his space head gear and returned to the shuttle's cleansing chamber. In this small room he placed his gear into several drawers, which appeared in the order he removed each item of clothing. They then shut automatically for screening, cleansing and re-packing.

His naked body was then exposed to a surrounding shower of soft water which was warmed to his body temperature. He remembered when he went through these exercises how his body was always sweaty and it was pleasing to have this space treatment. Since this was his first real life experience all he could feel was the tiny droplets hitting his body. He was not sweaty after his three hours outside and if anything he felt energetic and almost happy. He could not wait to have a debriefing with his commander – Tara. In an hour he was doing just that. Tara was businesslike in her task of evaluating his answers and the overall opinion was that there was nothing toxic to human life outside. Les would have to sleep in the isolation chamber for tonight in the nude and from time to time he would be checked by the others looking at the different monitors and by other automated equipment as his life signs will be compared to his health history profile. It may seem that this was excessive precautions taken but it was really a routine which had to be followed.

Les slept as the proverbial baby and there were no effects due to his exposure. Rather than completing more tests Tara made the decision with the others, that there tasks be broken down into the following for each to have more time with their specialities. Les will go look and record his findings on the flora and fauna of the planet. Len would look at the mineral make up of the planet and make plans on the location of mineral deposits, while Tara will try and look for water either on the surface or in underground streams. She also wanted them all to check for animal life especially avian life form, since she recorded trees with nuts and seeds apart from the large conifers which were in the majority of the forests. With all that food source around there must be some form of animal life. This little observation was noted and was shared with all so it was also part of their task to look for the same. If any form of animal life were seen, it was necessary to place out a contact call via the portable intercoms to which they were all attached. All contact would also be stored on the shuttle so it will also act as a contact communication source in case their signals were blocked from each other either by a physical structure, such as a mountain, valley or cave.

It was suggested that they all use the repository of the computer link on the shuttle at the end of each work day. Rations were packed, some emergency medical supplies and the usual solar cells etc. Each crew member had light packs to carry and they also had their scooters which folded in a rucksack type easy enough to carry. With a shake of hands Tara set out with a determined set to her jaw since she had to cover the whole planet which was approximately the size of earth. Len set out to tackle a North South circumference, while Les travelled in an East West direction.

The planet was covered by the three space cadets and that was not going to be a problem since the mother ship had ensured them that there were no animal life-forms on the planet. *The rest of this story covers only the exploits of Leslie Ram, the Stellar Microbiologist who was given the task of checking out the microscopic forms of both animal and plant life. It is here that a strange selection process appears to have taken place for he immediately felt at home with this planet. In fact, he said later on that he felt as though he belonged to the place. He also explained to the debriefing committee that there was something that he felt which was not picked up by any of their scans or their psychological inquiries. He felt first of all that they were all under some type of observation but which he felt intuitively was benign*

He had to explain that since there were no obvious signs of animal life form as shown by their distant scans, he should be free to explore on the ground like a camper back on earth. He felt safe in asking for this, as there was a probe that had been discharged and was hovering high above the planet. It was in an orbit that allowed the shuttle to have an 'mechanical eye' over the twenty four hour cycle of the planet. This cycle was comprised of a twelve hour day and night and could be monitored safely from their central location. He did not feel it necessary to record any of his thoughts on the subject. Indeed, he almost felt that it would be the wrong thing to record his personal feelings. He put it all down to being the first to leave the ship and to the absolute silence from mechanical noises that they were all used to. The loneliness of the area had a calming effect on him and mellowed his spirit.

For the first time he was aware of the total absence of the continual humming of the shuttle engines and also that of the parent ship. His hearing had to cope with a mild ringing sound due to the complete absence of mechanical sounds. His feeling of being observed was enhanced as soon as he left the shuttle to begin his mission. Before he entered the forest of trees, he stopped and looked as his colleagues just as they disappeared from sight, neither of whom turned to look back or to wave farewell.

Encounter with Proto

It was almost with some anticipation and more than an excitement that Les entered the glade in front of the shuttle. When he turned around to look back at the shuttle and to set the co ordinates for the position of his locator the craft looked so lonely and small to him. He smiled to himself and began to walk and look at the trees around him. Their heights were phenomenal, three hundred feet some twice that size. His recorders soon revealed a temperate type forest with lots of evergreens and few deciduous but what had caught his attention was the size of their leaves, which measured two to three metres across on trees similar to the umbrella trees. The pine and fir trees were straight and had girths of two to three metres at their base but he soon saw some even larger ones as he continued his stroll through this majestic garden of Eden. He also noted that the ground was soft to his tread because of a continuous carpet of cottony fir and pine needles. There was the occasional small bush like scrub at the base of these shaded trees but they too appeared to be lush with a dark green leaves and a soft main stem.

His analyser showed that the chlorophyll was similar to that of the programmed control, with a slight accentuation in the amount of red type, which was not obvious as he looked at the few deciduous trees around. He smiled as he breathed in deeply and thought to himself that this place must be the most colourful when the autumn comes along – if indeed there was an autumn...

Leslie stood under the canopy of the monster size trees and made a video recording of all that was around him. He stopped and went over to look closely at the trunk of the trees, which was smooth, free of the normal longitudinal bark scorings common to the pine and spruce trees. It was as though they had the clean smooth feel of the Australian Gum trees. He also noted that some of the same trees also had different coloured bark, some with the accepted brown colour while others had a ghost blue-white colour. Then as his video was recording his observations he felt more than ever that there were eyes looking at him. He looked up at the trees but his feelings were not terrifying but he felt that he was being observed, quietly by unseen eyes. He spun around quickly to look between the trees, then he looked up at the cavernous canopy and realised that his mind was probably playing tricks on him. None of his analysers showed activity of animal or humanoid forms present. He left his analyser on permanent search in case he might miss a signal. He had readjusted his scanner again for animal even microbial life forms and was satisfied that his monitors were all working correctly.

It was strange that he could still see the sunlight dancing in between the trees in spite of the thick foliage of the branches and the canopy. The quietness of the forest was eerie since he could only hear his blood pumping through the carotid arteries near to his eardrum. There has been a small medical problem which Leslie had and it was a genetic fault. His parents and school personnel did not feel necessary to have it surgically fixed. Even when at rest Leslie's blood pressure would be elevated to the abnormal level for men of his age. Leslie did not tell anyone but as he got older he realised that he just had an abnormally high blood pressure when at rest.

The medical staff did place a small monitor under his right rib cage with a small dose cartridge which would inject a beta blocker if his BP went to abnormal levels not contiguous with his personal range. The microchip had the history of his medical file, which was continually checked as a back ground by the mother ship analysers dealing with the staff health. As a result, he had his own personal case history on him with his normal values with which to compare.

As he continued to walk through this soft carpet of pine, fir and spruce needles, he did not see any twigs, or fallen leaves and he did not get close enough to touch the trees. It appeared as though these could have been a crop of equally spaced trees which were kept by an army of personnel for nothing appeared to be out of order. He looked at his watch and realised that he had been walking and recording his surroundings for almost three hours and it was nutrition time but he did not feel like eating. His mouth was not even dry and his breathing was slow and relaxed he felt under his armpit for any dampness and it felt dry. He thought that maybe his sweat was been taken up by the air. What did fit in was his lack of water intake for he did not feel thirsty. However, through his training he withdrew his flask of liquid drink and took a swig.

Normally, he would have held the flask to his lips and have a long drink allowing the sweetish fluid to fill the back of his throat before he removed it from his lips. Indeed he would have three to four such drinks if he was on the ship before he replaced the flask. As it was the one swig was all he had and as if in a daze he replaced the stopper and slid the flask into his shoulder pack.

He continued to walk forward but he drifted and had to blink his eyes several times to clear his vision, he felt as though he was staggering after an evening of drinking too much wine. He settled himself and began to place one foot in front of the other. It was still bright day light and he thought that he had approximately four more hours of daylight. He looked around him and felt a bit woozy again then he saw an opening in the trees ahead. He headed in that direction to catch the sight of the sun in this clearing. His staggering appeared to have left him but he had a feeling of euphoria again similar to having a few glasses of wine. He began to smile to himself and fleetingly thought that maybe Tara was playing a joke by replacing the nutrient solution with some wine. He took out the bottle and held his analyser next to it and sure enough it read nutrient solution. There was no indication of alcohol present other than the basic nutrients that were prepared for all external staff outings from the ship.

Ah!, he laughed then it must be the air, too much natural oxygen in lungs accustomed only to manufactured breathing air of the parent ship of which he was a worker for the past five years. That is what is making me heady he laughed loudly to himself and he was startled when the sound of his laughter echoed back at twice the decibels as was released. Ha! There must be a wall or obstacle nearby which is acting like an echo chamber. He picked up the pace making for the sunlight opening which he saw just ahead of him but after awhile he let out a loud "Helloooo" only to wait for almost 10 seconds and have it ricochet back at least fifty times louder. It hurt his ears and he placed his hands over the pinna and ran into the opening which was only a small patch of grass covered area not more than a hundred metres square. He stopped and looked up at the sun above, which was beginning to slant towards the western sky. His head settled and he drew in a deep breath and as if by magic his senses were alert. He looked high into the canopy of the tree nearest him and he thought that his eyes were playing tricks for he thought that there was a green head looking down at him with large brown eyes with a green face and hair, revealing a smile on its branched shaped face. It was similar to looking at the clouds in a blue sky, where one could see faces of monsters or giants and other things. He looked down and across the verge of the grass at the red bark on the trees similar to the Sequoia, but these were not like those recorded on Earth two thousand years previously. He went over to the trees and as he packed away his recorders and other gadgets he put out a hand to touch the smooth bark and to his utter surprise, it was as though he had touched another human skin.

It was soft and warm and appeared to allow him to keep his hand on its trunk as he stroked it for it was comforting to him as well. Oh my goodness! What type of tree are you, he thought to himself. It is not something that he had ever experienced and he thought that he would collect some samples the next day and do a quick DNA analysis for the records. When he removed his hands, a mist of small pollen like dust appeared to drop out of the branches. Leslie looked up and saw the microscopic mist of pollen grains dropping aimlessly on him and around him and then he felt for the first time a small cool breeze brush at his naked face. Leslie did not tie up the fact that his stroking the bark of the tree and the pollen grains as well as, the wind as being connected in any way. Again he had a quick glance at his watch and looked up at the clear blue sky which was changing to a dark blue as the sun began to slope away and thought that this was just as good a place to stay as any. So he began to unpack his small tent and to make preparations for sleep for he was feeling quite relaxed. He extracted a damp wipe for his face, armpits and groin area. He also thought that it was time to urinate but he did not feel the urge for any toilet relief. His body needed to acclimatise itself to a terrain existence, he thought to himself.

As in his training ritual, he automatically set up his communicator antennae and laid out his bed pack for the night. He stored the wet wipe into his small garbage container and lay his scooter pack on the ground unopened. He placed his tent near to the tree which he had stroked and thought that he would use the slight hump at the root as an elevation for his pillow. Again Leslie looked at his rations but did not feel like any food at all. He thought that he would scout around to look for some source of water as the silence did not betray any sound of water fall or streams or rivers as been close to where he was. These giant trees needed a lot of moisture to produce all this organic material

There must be huge underground rivers or aquifers or the roots of these trees must burrow very deep indeed to draw up moisture necessary for the formation of all this cytoplasm in the leaves, the flowers and fruit cones which appear at the end of the pine and spruce branches. There was little or no humidity in the atmosphere to nurture this gargantuan forest.

As Leslie settled down to his light chores which was part of an automatic behaviour as a result of a training ritual which he has had to do for as long as he could remember, he thought how lucky they were to have stumbled onto this biblical Garden of Eden. These very large great trees which appear to form a cathedral ceiling over four to five hundred metres high, with the unusual bark appear to be very healthy and clean. There were no crevices for insects to hide and feed that were available.

That was the other notable fact the total lack of insects, so these plants must be all fertilised by wind. But even the wind was limited to a sub sensitive level just enough to keep his skin cool and relaxed. Again he looked at the trees and mentally noted the presence of trees similar to the cedar, birches which had a pure white smooth bark, appeared as though they were white washed with a bright white paint and the slight ripple or hum from a poplar tree were all that he could superficially record. As far as, he could detect there were little suspended organic material and no microbes were detected in the air. If there is a lot of organic material suspended in the atmosphere then there tended to be even more microbes also suspended, since they ride the wind on the flying carpets of dust and other organic material. Bird sounds would have completed this paradise that he was enjoying.

Les intended to take samples of dirt, organic soil material, take specimens from as many trees as possible and to take his time doing the DNA typing and cataloguing in the next few days. He felt that he should make preparations for the night. He knew from their earlier monitoring that the temperature would not change much in the night and he was sure that with the low humidity there would be little risk of inclement weather. He settled down surrounding himself with monitors, communication links on alert and decided to just lay down under the azure blue sky and dream a bit.

A quick check of his surrounded paraphernalia brought a sense of incongruity and shock to him for the first time his little collection of devices looked so limited and insignificant. He knew that when he eventually nodded off these instruments would download wirelessly into his shuttle's computer. However, he let the thought pass away just as quickly as it came to him. He did feel the urge to remove his foot wear and heavy trousers and upper shirt. He laid them out in an orderly mosaic on the floor of his tent. He placed another ground sheet on the ground outside his tent and when he lay on it, there was a feeling of softness as though he was lying on a mattress of cotton. He smiled to himself and said loudly as though he was talking to fellow campers, "well tonight I shall camp out doors, since I have never done this before it will be for my personal diary"

He touched the two transparent patches on the ground sheet and a soft light glowed and as it got darker, his light looked soft and comforting. His whole body began to feel a cool glow for his skin had not been exposed to anything other than to the artificial environment of their space ships. As the day light disappeared, he was aware of a sweet odour just in the air. He walked up to his pillow tree and sure enough there was a stronger odour coming from his tree. It was invigorating and he reached out to stroke the strong smooth bark again.

To his surprise the whole tree appeared to shudder to his minuscule stroking. He laughed and try to push it harder but the feeling on his naked hand was like pushing the muscle of his wrestling friend when he worked out. He stopped turned around and leaned against the trunk, slowly sliding down to a sitting position. Again there was a slight shower of pollen and a cool breeze which moved the upper leaves and blew against his face and bare legs. It was soothing and he felt the need to just rest but he knew that he had a silly smile on his face.

He reached out and turned off the communicator next to his ground sheet for he could feel its throb. He thought I shall contact the others in the morning for I need a good rest tonight. He had covered over 25 kilometres today very easily and his recorders and monitors were documenting his every move. A quick and automatic look at his time locator, showed it to be early evening and he still did not feel the need for either water or food. As he lay down and looked up at the now deep twilight, unusual clusters of stars began to show in the distance.

This was also comforting since he was always surrounded by night time and stars for most of his working life. That strange and delightful breeze again appeared to stay close to his body rendering a delightful languor which brought on a pleasant drowsiness. As sleep came on him he reached out for his defender laser weapon and dragged it close to his chest. He smiled and thought of how stupid this action was but his conditioned training just made this a reflex action. Les lay on his back and had a last look at the covering branches of his protective tree and from that position he noticed the large swellings of cone-like structures hanging at the end of each branch. From this vantage they seem to appear larger but it just could be that with the darkness now in the canopy, everything did appear to have a larger attachment shadow. With this thought he was fast asleep.

Les felt his eyes open first before he moved. He was aware that he was quite alert but did not move his hand felt the security of the laser comforting on his side. He continued to breathe regularly as if he was still asleep. It was still night but it was a bright night and this in itself was odd since there were no other circulating moons which would have reflected the light of the single sun and the stars were several million light years away to have little or no effect in providing any light. From this foetal position, he looked around through slitted eyes at his surroundings and all appeared to be the same, but there was a continuous breeze which was still providing a soft kiss to the skin only now it was continuous. The sweet smell of the evening was replaced by a distinct lavender one just as pleasant to the senses. His monitors were still on as was his bed sheet light. He slowly shifted his weight and stretched out rolling onto his back, keeping his eyes slitted. This gave the impression of total relaxation. He looked down towards his feet and through the V shape of his feet which was pointed towards the open grassy patch, which now appeared yellow golden in this bright twilight. He thought that it must be the reflection of his monitor lights but they were so dim and could not have given such a bright colour reflection.

CONTACT

Leslie found that his hearing was acute with that peculiar slight ringing which was as a result of the total absence of sound. However, something did wake him up and he was trying to remember what it was. As he lay on his back looking through slit eyes, he glanced up at the trees above and he could still see the canopy even the colour which was darker but still definable. However, he noted the concs at the end of each branch appeared much larger, actually a lot larger and he still thought that it must be a trick of the darkness.

He slowly sat up stretched and looked up at the patch of stars in the still dark night. He cautiously rose to a standing position and as he turned around away from the forest to the grassy verge he stopped transfixed for he thought that there was something out of place. He looked hard at the edge furthest away from him and thought that there were small thin trees which were not there earlier. He moved in that direction to examine closer but as he neared the spot, a wind blew around him and the trees rustled. He thought that the small tree was an apparition which appeared to walk away from him or so he thought.

He turned around quickly to his stack of gear and picked up a portable light to shine in the direction of the small tree or at what he had imagined he had seen. It was not there as the yellow beam of light just reflected off the yellow grass. He moved forward again to check out the spot at the edge of the grass verge and there were no small trees but he could now discern a path in the grass so he began to follow it. Looking down to make sure that he was on the path, he cautiously proceeded to search for any obstacles in the path. As he raised the light to peer ahead he thought he saw a shadow ahead. It was bipedal but very thin and it was moving from one shadow spot to the other away from him.

He shouted "Hello wait!" But the apparition moved rapidly away in the dark. Then there was the loud echo of his voice booming back to him. It sent shivers along the back of his neck. He stopped and thought was this fear, that he was feeling for this was alien to him.

As he peered into the darkness moving his light from side to side there was nothing he could see. He fixed the light on a clump of grasses which he had not seen the previous day but now he was in new territory. He moved up to it and had a scan around and could only see shadows. This is useless looking in the dark and as he turned around to retrace his steps putting it all down to an active imagination, he caught a movement out of the corner of his eye and there was movement right next to him. He flashed his light in the direction suddenly and saw a humanoid form leap up to its height of near enough two metres tall, thin brown but what astounded him was the size of its eyes. They were large round white corneas with large brown irises. It looked at him and moved with remarkable speed as though skimming above the surface of the ground. He focussed his light at the departing humanoid form and began to give chase and not looking at the path, which opened into a grass plain.

Leslie was panting a bit by now in the excitement and kept calling "Wait, Hello, don't run away. Hello I am friendly" He was fast losing ground to the departing figure and he felt for his laser, which he withdrew while on the run and decided to fire above the head of the fast moving figure. It discharged with a loud hiss and showed a flare, where he could see the lank form bend down close to the ground and was scooting low to the ground. His sounds along with the discharge echoed back with such a velocity that he felt himself slide to the ground and rolled over as though pushed from behind. He let out a yelp as he felt his ankle twist under his weight. He knew that he broke his ankle for he had never felt pain like this before. He tried to sit up and when he shone the light he could see the angle of his leg and he immediately knew that it was bad. The pain was excruciating, his laser gun had fallen out of his hand. "Well that was a lovely way to meet folks in a new planet. I have also dropped my guard and not followed orders and training so this is how failed missions occur" he said loudly.

Leslie began to feel sorry for himself as the pain of his broken ankle began to take all his attention. Every move to straighten his leg and to sit up in a comfortable position brought on sharp pains. He had no foot cover, a small pair of pants and a summer shirt reminiscent of a vacation summer wear. His laser was lost all he had,was his light and his body monitor. He was so involved looking at his ankle and pulling himself up into a sitting position, that he did not see the figure standing next to him. He turned around and shone the light into the face of a thin, humanoid figure that had no artificial vestment covering his torso. Its eyes were large, its head square with rounded edges. Its arms were spindly ending in three long finger-like appendages. It looked back at Leslie sitting on the ground and reached down to gently push the light away from its face. Leslie shouted in panic "who are you? Can you speak to me?" The figure ignored his talking and reached for his ankle before he could say much more, he felt a pleasant sound purring in his head. He looked at the gentle tri finger with no nails holding his dangling ankle and realised that it knew he was hurt and was trying to help him

Leslie again heard the purring sound in his head then sounds appeared to come into his minds – words, yes words. "Ah! You are telepathic" The brown head bobbed up and down and a finger was placed over its small thin mouth. Leslie caught on, he must be making too much noise so he focussed his thoughts into the first question, "Who are you?"

The purring sound came again as he heard "You will know all soon. Please stay quiet while I heal your broken appendage"

Before he could inquire as to how it would be done, two soft fingers were placed on his temples and he felt himself relax. He closed his eyes but could only feel his legs straighten out and he was gently pushed into a prostrate position. He found that he could not open his eyes but he was also relaxed and his pain had disappeared.

SEE NO EVIL

Leslie awoke as if from a deep sleep and either by his training or from a practised habit, his eyes opened first before he moved. He quickly recalled his chase and meeting the strange biped then he furtively reached down to feel his ankle and as he carefully flexed it, there did not appear to be any problem. Did I dream this whole episode? He thought to himself. He was on his ground sheet but his position was not against the tree with the warm bark but in the middle of the dense forest under the huge compact canopy. He relaxed from his foetal sleeping position and rolled onto his back. He then sat up and looked around and about him. As he surveyed his position, there was a pleasant buzzing in his head and words came to him, "Halloo! Are you feeling better?"

He stood up and whirled around and could see nothing but the trunks of the trees with the dappled sunlight playing about the high branches.

He relaxed and closed his eyes, "Yes, I am. Where are you?"

"Would you like to see me?" was the reply.

"Yes, I really would and thanks for healing my foot," he replied. He was getting the hang of speaking his thoughts by this very pleasant telepathic form.

"Is your name Leslie Ram?" asked the inquisitive buzz in his head.

"Why yes! That is what I am called" he replied. Leslie noted that the buzz was no longer the lead into the conversation.

"What is your name?" he quickly added and :"where are you?" Les asked as he kept turning and looking around.

"I am called Proto, hee, hee" was the very pleasant reply. Les could not believe that he heard a giggle in his head.

"Do you always have so many questions in your head all the time?" asked Proto."Hee, hee, hee"

Les began to laugh to himself as he continued to move around and look in all the passages through the trees.

"I apologise for my inquisitive behaviour and curiosity but I am on a mission to look at your planet" as he bent down to pick up both an analyser and hand held scanner. They were both dead. They were completely non-functioning. He laid them down and for the first time he felt helpless.

"Your things do not respond?" asked the voice in his head.

"Yes they appear to be non-functioning. I do not understand why since I checked them out last evening and they were fine" replied Les trying to keep the dialogue going.

"Hee, Hee, I did that, " replied Proto.

"Oh! You did that" laughed Les nervously.

"Why did you damage my equipment" he cautiously inquired.

"They are not damaged" replied Proto. " But your thing made a lot of noise, so we made them quiet, Hee, hee." He continued.

"What thing?" then, Leslie remembered firing off his laser gun over the head of Proto in his chase.

"Proto, I did not mean to hurt you I just wanted you to stop and meet with me. I am truly sorry and please accept my apology." Leslie was truly apologetic.

There was a silence then a slow buzz came into his head again but no sound. Les raised his head and asked "Proto are you still there? Please accept my apology."

"I really did not mean to hurt you or anyone else. I just wanted to make contact since I thought that there were only trees present on this planet, so your appearance startled me. I am truly sorry for my hasty action."

"My scanner did not detect your presence, Proto," continued Leslie. He had a feeling that he was losing contact and whirled around again looking around him.

"I know that you meant no harm to Proto and his family and I also know that your family is also safe to be with us," replied Proto.

"Have you contacted my other friends, Proto? Are they all right?" asked Leslie with some concern. There was a long pause before the reply came from Proto.

"In answer to your question, we have not made contact with your family. Secondly, they appear to be all right and have shown great interest in the ecosystem of our home. In your words, they are OK Hee, hee."

Proto continued, preventing Leslie from asking another question, "We thought that it was best to make contact with only you since you have shown warmth to our brethren by stroking them and showing affection to them." Leslie had no idea of what he had done to get such a response from Proto and thought better than to ask what it was. Besides he was getting quite accustomed to this form of mental communication, which he found to be exhilarating.

"Proto where are you I cannot see you and I am looking around for a focus from where your thoughts are coming. Is there a problem that you are hiding from me? Why did you choose to contact only me and not my colleagues, Oh! I mean my family?" was the earnest inquiry from Leslie.

There was a long pause before a reply came "Les ..lie, you have too many thoughts floating in your mind. We will answer all your questions and what you wish to know ......only do not use your vocal ..... apparatus for it startles.... my, our...family," came Proto's response.

To Leslie this response appeared laboured as if Proto was receiving instructions from a third party. He could also feel a background buzz in the back of his mind but he could not concentrate to decipher any significant thought. Maybe this was the equivalent of whispering in telepathy. He could however, feel himself mastering this form of communication and for some unknown reason to him, it was like he was at junior school again and learning something new.

He could feel an excitement of achievement and he knew that he would pass this test. It was a strange and pleasant feeling of youth learning quickly and becoming confident and wants to move ahead more quickly. This was how it was when he was in junior school and had a mind like a sponge and when everyday was exciting for there was something new to learn and master, when he was a boy. It appears that Proto through his telepathy subliminal coaching of Les, had dug deep into his sub conscious and chosen to awake the same youthful learning ability with it's corresponding endorphin stimulation This in turn led to this excitement that he was feeling for the first time in a long time. There was the total lack of fear and apprehension at what he was experiencing, and he loved every minute that he had spent Tele-communicating with Proto. He tried several times to think of the logical protocol to follow when meeting a new species. It appeared that all his training had vanished and he had to find out as much as possible. He felt for his personal attached recorder, which was attached to his inside shirt and pressed onto his chest. He had a quick glance at this monitor and saw the dim light on so he felt that all will be recorded and so he did not have to worry about following any set protocol. These thoughts raced through his mind and he wondered if they were being interpreted by his unseen contact.

He called out mentally, "Proto are you still there? "Yes Les...lie right behind you" Leslie turned around with a start only to see the full sight of his contact. He was astonished and startled. In broad daylight, Proto was as tall as he was which was near enough six feet but he had little bulk. Narrow shoulders, skin brown and smooth, his most prominent feature was the box-like head with those huge brown eyes which were so expressive. His feet also ended in three toes which did not have any nails. They were clubbed toes with a flat sole. He had no sex organs between his legs. His mouth was a very small slit and where his nose should be were two small holes on a very small promontory. He had no ears with a pinna, just two small holes at the side of his huge head, relative to the rest of his body. His eyes moved up from time to time to the top of his cornea when he was communicating with Les.

"Oh! You startled me, Proto. Can you make yourself invisible? Were you behind me all the time?" asked the excited Les.

"Too many questions too fast. Sorry Les...lie, for startling you. No, and No.. Hee...hee," Proto's eyes went up as though he was laughing.

Les laughed and kept a smile on his face then continued "Oh Proto !, I am so excited to meet you especially when I or we thought that there was no animal life much less humanoid form on the planet, just these beautiful, magnificent trees. Our scanners must be malfunctioning for we would have prepared differently to meet with your people."

71

"In fact we would not have landed on the planet since it is our policy not to contact alien life forms for fear of being misinterpreted as being invaders," continued the excited Leslie.

"Les...lie, slow down. We were with you always. Your scan...ner did not mal..function. We did not wish to be seen so we stayed in our ..hive ..eh..home," responded Proto.

"Shh.. Let me continue Les..lie. Look at my ..our family they are also excited to meet you. Would you like to meet our family, Les..lie?."

Leslie beamed at this brown face with the laughing eyes. "Oh Proto, I would love to meet you family and to see your hive, if you will lead the way."

"Les..lie there is no way to go, look at the trees, our hive," and he pointed to the trunks of the trees.

Leslie was startled for from every tree bodies separated from the trunk of the trees like plastecine and before his eyes each tree was surrounded by so many of Proto-like forms that soon the forest was full of these bodies forming a circle of several individuals deep. There was also a sweet smell of lavender and spice filling the air around Proto and Leslie.. Then his head began to buzz, as Proto raised his three fingered skinny arm – all heads were immediately bowed and only one voice was telepathically transmitted.

"It is good to meet you ..Les..lie. Welcome to our hive and our family. We will show you all you wish to know."

Les looked at Proto who had kept watching Leslie throughout this latter communication, with his eyes looking up to the top of his head then down in a most expressive way. They were kind eyes.

Proto looked directly at him and said "Les..lie, it is better if only one communicates with you. If the whole family communicates at the same time – ah mm, Hee ..hee your head would be hurt. You cannot take this stress right now, maybe after some time..."

"Proto the trees, are they your home ah hive?" asked the startled Les.

"Hee...hee no Les..lie, we are the trees and the trees are us" replied Proto. "I will show you how we are one in one, but later."

"You need to rest," said Proto and from the crowd a little whistle arose like that of a twit sparrow, soft and melodious. From the top of the trees, a light dust of pollen descended on all of them and they all opened their little slit of mouths and inhaled this dust. Leslie looked up and opened his mouth and stuck out his tongue to trap some of this pollen.

This was observed by the mass of beings and then the buzz began in his head first like a laugh then like an overwhelming roar which made him dizzy and as he looked around him at all the little slits with pink insides all staring at him, he felt faint and turned to Proto whose eyes opened even wider appeared to be concerned and he raised his hand. The family immediately bent their heads and the sound of the buzzing stopped immediately.

"We are sorry Les..lie, the family thought that you looked funny sticking out the lip in your mouth and they all wanted to ... laugh, like you. It was too much it will not happen again. You must rest."

As Les turned around, he was amazed at how quickly all the life forms attached and literally melted into the trees. In less than a minute there was only Proto and himself.

Les looked at the pleasant face of his host Proto and asked "Proto what is the name of your people or race who lives in the tree?"

Again those laughing eyes," We are called Proto and this is the Birthplace," Proto simply replied."You rest now and we will show you how we live in the Birthplace"

Leslie was beginning to feel quite relaxed and indeed he felt as though he could crash on the soft floor of needles and just go to sleep. Instead, he went to his ground sheet near one of the trees walking with Proto, who was pointing him towards it and then Proto said "Les..lie, you will sleep at my hive" as he pointed to the tree where his tent and ground sheet was laid out. Les thought that Proto would just melt into his head pillow tree and smiled at the thought. He had hardly sat down when he turned to the nearby Proto, yawned looked at him and said "It does not look like night time as yet but I am very tired and sleepy. Thank you for all you have done today. You are very lovely folks" He rolled onto his sheet and was fast asleep. Proto looked at him, shifted his eyes up then melted into the tree.

HEAR NO EVIL

Leslie could not remember any of his dreams as he opened his eyes through slitted lids. He cautiously tried to recall all that he thought he had seen yesterday or was it all just a dream. He looked from his foetal position at the forest opposite from him and all he could see were trees and the dappled sunlight filtering through the upper branches. He rolled over onto his back and was shocked to see Proto sitting at his back with those large expressive eyes, he was jolted but smiled and sat up immediately. Proto stood up and began to walk away, Leslie followed and he found that he was light on his feet and very energetic. "Sorry Proto, I must have over slept. Were you waiting long for me to arise?" asked Les with a bright smile.

Proto also moved his smiling eyes and said "Proto did not wait for you to awake, Les..lie. I have brought you to the Birthplace, so that all will be explained to you," he continued.

"Ha Proto! You have brought me or you will take me to the Birthplace" replied Les with his beaming smile. He was pleased that all he could remember did happen and he had met with this new species.

"No Proto brought you to the Birthplace" and pointed to the back of Les, who turned around to see the most fantastic site before him. He was never here last evening and he turned enquiring eyes back to Proto. Before he could ask the obvious question, Proto placed one of his digits to his small slit of a mouth. Les realised that he would be told everything especially how they transported him and his little cluster of space paraphernalia without waking him. While it would have torn at his mind as to how they did he just was so full of enthusiasm and goodwill that he turned and followed Proto to the site of one of the greatest trees that anyone could have imagined. They were looking at the largest Sequoia with a width that blanketed his vision so he thought he was staring at a huge red wooden trunk, which obstructed their path with no end in sight. He looked up at the canopy of the tree, with massive branches extending for hundreds of feet in the air covered such a massive area that there were no other trees which could be seen anywhere around. This one tree was a forest to itself. He stepped back to look upwards and could not see the top because of the branches which were letting the sunshine in to lighten up the whole mass.

His neck was straining as he ran first to the right and turned to Proto with questioning eyes then he raced along the roots to the left. He just could not bring the whole monstrous size tree into any perspective. He returned to where Proto was standing and he heard a sharp buzz which startled him as his head sharply turned with a reflex towards Proto, whose head was bowed. He reached over to touch Proto for the first time and he felt a warm smooth skin give under his touch. Proto raised up his head and his eyes were smiling and moving up and down in his huge big head as though they were not under control. Les quickly moved his hand and Proto's eyes began to settle down in his face.

"Sorry Proto, were you praying to the mother tree, Ah Birthplace," Les was confused.

Proto began to mimic Les giggle "Do not distress yourself, Les.. lie, you Hee ...hee.. tickled me when you touched me. It made me excited for your touch is very, very..stimulating to us. It was told to us the first time you touched our hive where you slept the first night. So we all know what your touch is like. Later I shall pass your touch to all the family, thank you Les..lie., I must now try to answer some of your questions. Close your eyes and let me explain."

Proto moved closer to the root of the giant red wood and they sat on the root ridge. Les sat down and immediately closed his eyes.

A pleasant buzz began in the front of his head then went to the mid of his brain. It then changed into a sweet lullaby like song

"Leslie," came the soft voice. "The trees and Proto are one and the same. Look at my branches and you will see the large round fruits hanging at the end of my branches. These are the new Proto which will be fertilised this

evening. We are trees but we are the Proto also. When you touch the trunk of the tree, you touch us the Proto. Your hands are warm and it is pleasing to us. If you did not touch the bark of the tree or stroked it we would never have shown ourselves to you. But we searched your mind when you were asleep and we found that you did not bear us harm. We wanted to make contact since you wished to take samples from us. That would have destroyed some of our family. Your friends also want samples so we have given them some of our departed Proto. I will ask that you follow what Proto ask you to do for you will see the reason for our existence as well as your existence. Your questions will be answered – have patience. Proto will hold Leslies appendage and show him our role in the universe. Leslie keep your eyes shut and all will be projected into your mind –trust us."

Leslie nodded a positive or agreeable assent and then wondered if they understood what a nod meant. He smiled to himself and he relaxed totally. Through his slitted eyelids, he held out his hands to Proto, whose finger barely touched his. They then both began to rise up the slope of the tree and he noted Proto's digit on the other hand just barely touching the trunk of the great red Sequoia. It was if they were in an old fashion elevator described in the old text books of the twenty second century on his home planet earth. They both rose up the sheer trunk of the great red and settled several hundred feet above the ground on a branch which had the width for ten of their shuttle craft to park comfortable next to each other. The finger digit contact with Proto separated as they settled on their feet. Proto pointed to the edge of the smaller sub branches and then to the giant leaves and finally to the large globular round fruiting bodies each about the size of two soccer balls. They were brown and looked soft as they bobbed slightly. They both stood comfortably where they could see the rest of the forest in the distance. Les could also see a large savannah grass covered plain out through the branches. He could also see the sunshine bright as ever and even the swaying of the large green to yellow golden grass. This was different from what he had been seeing for the last few days.

There was a creaking sound as if the whole tree was shuddering but only just slightly. A wind came up it was gentle and cool to the skin. He was still inspecting the height of the tree and the massive branches which could have supported the rail system used in the mother ship to move personnel and supplies around. It was strange that he made such an analogy to the mother ship for he was watching a tree, which was a huge forest in its own rite but was almost as big indeed several times bigger than the mother ship. This mother ship carried over one thousand men, women with supplies of food, water and parts for the shuttles and probes enough to remain in space for over ten years. Granted when the opportunity presented itself to take on supplies then the mother ship availed itself to do so but this was a rare occurrence.

In the midst of his mental rambling he felt a touch on his arm and Proto told him to sit down on the branch. Just as they both had sat down, there was another stronger breeze which appears to persist and from this vantage point. Les could see and hear the leaves tinkling or rustling above and around them He could also hear the hard rubbing of the branches as they were pitched against each other but this only occurred at the ends of the forks of the giant red tree, which hardly showed any effect of this wind. He did see the fruiting globes swinging at the ends of the ultimate branches. Then Proto pointed out beyond the tree at a mass of small white umbrella-like seedlings blowing in the wind headed for the Sequoia. Proto appeared to be excited while Les could not quite understand the reason as it just appeared that some tree had just discharged it's flowers on their umbrella like parachute apparatus so that they could fall elsewhere and germinate. Earth's botany was not quite what he had expected but it was rather close. As they both watched intently at the horde of white umbrellas approach, two things were apparent first they were moving positively towards their tree and secondly this was not random distribution, for it appears as if the Sequoia was actually setting up the breeze or wind to bring these botanical bodies towards its branches.

It was not long before the upper branches mainly at the end with the leaves and globule like fruit were having these umbrella forms attached to each and everyone. As soon as the umbrella form was attached to the round brown fruit it was adsorbed onto and into the fruiting body. Another amazing observation was that there were no spare globule or left over umbrella seeds. Every one of the umbrella forms were used. Proto touched Les's arm and they both stood up as a huge earthquake like shudder rocked the giant tree. It only lasted for a brief few seconds but threw them both on their backsides. The big brown eyes of Proto danced as though he was truly happy. He reached out to touch digit to finger and Les did as he was told and closed his eyes. He could feel them elevate and then begin to descend and it was not long before they were on the ground Proto beckoned him to follow for he had a determined look about him which was not observed before. As they went along the back side of the tree which was on the opposite side to where they had began, Les could see the grassy plains in the distance away from the massive trunk of the tree.

Proto lead them away from the tree towards the field of swaying grasses. For the first time, Les felt he had to extend himself physically to keep up with the fast moving or gliding Proto who was intent in moving forward with some urgency. This was not the time to ask any questions as Les knew that he was receiving answers to questions as he went along. After about thirty minutes of a most harried walk, they came to the verge of the grassy plains and Les was taken back at the height of the grass which was indeed golden but the reeds were five to six feet tall. Proto turned around and pointed back at the tree.

At this distance the top branches of the tree were still extended just beyond their sight. Les turned in the direction of the pointed digit just in time to see a greatly enhanced size of the globules or fruiting body. The fruits were expanding into large circular bodies. Then a magnificent site took place as these huge suspended fruiting bodies transformed the huge tree into a large decorated Christmas tree with these suspended bodies dominating the size of the upper branches. Then the wind, as if by some defined signal, Les was beginning to be aware, began to skim across the grass with more of a force than he had ever felt before. It just could be that he was in the open for the first time and could feel its force. They had to anchor themselves as it was coming from their back across the grassy plains swaying the grass reeds and making a swishing sound. They felt as the force of the wind passed by and around them to cascade up the huge tree and almost at a signal, the fruiting bodies which were now over four feet in diameter began to fall to the ground.

Les would have imagined that they would have broken, 'like a ripe melons' as they hit the ground. On the contrary the huge brown bladders hit the soft needle covered carpeted ground which was everywhere, they just laid there not even bouncing or rolling. It was if these 'boulder' like shapes were being caught by the carpeted ground. He observed that as they hit the ground there were no reverberations or shock as some of these fell just in front of where they were standing. He went forward to touch one which was just six feet away from him, Proto made no effort to prevent him.

He could see the soft smooth brown surface and when he touched them, they were warm and soft. Like the bark of the tree which he had touched the very first day he went into the forest, the sensation was the same. But in the sunshine these soft to the touch bodies began to harden into almost granite like hardness. Les found this speeded up process similar to the formation of spores in botany and in fungal microbes. This process occurred when there were adverse conditions such as the absence of water or extreme conditions, when "microscopic forms of life sporulates" to protect themselves. This was all part of his basic training where he dealt with the microscopic forms of life not with huge trees.

The analogy was the same with one exception, the planet and environment was still lush with some concealed water, sunlight and all the trees and vegetation appeared to be healthier than ever. He turned to see that Proto was keenly observing his actions with those large laughing eyes.

Before he could phrase a thought to ask what he had in mind, Proto placed a single digit to his slit of a mouth and Les heard the following:

"Les..lie, you do understand much about other forms of life. Proto and his family use this method to extend our family. Inside these eggs are small Proto which are developing into big Proto and then into trees when they are ready. This crop of Proto will not stay with us for they have a new job to do. The soft shell hardens quickly to protect the young Proto. We are happy for there are a lot more Proto formed more than we have ever had in my life time which in your time is over one hundred and fifty years. These baby Proto, in their eggs will be collected by us" and he pointed behind Les who turned around to see a mass of Proto descend into the fields from under the great tree and began to roll these 'eggs' towards the grassy plains, which was in their direction. Proto again interrupted Les thought and said "let us look from above and get out of the way." The whole process was being carried out with absolutely no noise or confusion. He turned to touch the extended digit of Proto and closed his eyes; he felt the gentle elevation and ascendance

above the ground. His legs were dangling but for some unknown reason he felt safe, as though he would not fall. Proto said "Les..lie, open your eyes and look down" Just by the touching of Les hands they were suspended over fifty feet above the ground. Les could see as Proto showed him, this field which was very vast hid hundreds if not thousands of these boulders strewn throughout the plains. These newly formed ones were added by the mass of Proto below who were rolling them into the grass and returning back into the forest. Les watched fascinated by the spectacle below him. He felt them begin to descend just outside the grassy plains.

When they were back on the ground, without any communication, Proto turned and set a rapid pace. Les picked up the pace to follow him back into the forest. It was quite a walk and from time to time, Les looked at the Proto who were also walking rapidly into the forest. Some were pale cream coloured, others were white to grey in colour, while there were a few yellow ones, others red and a few really black ones. Some had different coloured eyes ranging from different shades of brown to green and blue while others had almost red corneas. For the first time in daylight Les saw the population of this planet. As this moving crowd of Proto entered the forest they seemed to just disappear. He could see a few attach themselves to trees but they just vanished until only Proto and he were standing alone under the 'mother tree.'

Les found himself understanding these life forms and he also found that all he had was just wonder for what he had just witnessed. A strange affection for these beings was developing for they were turning out to be far superior to his species. His scientific mind just kicked in and thought that this was just a different form of evolution, which after all just fitted into his training in biology. He was becoming comfortable with this explanation to himself. He looked up at the huge canopy of the red wood tree, which appeared even more vast with the absence of the fruiting bodies. Proto had remained very quiet on the return trip, almost pensive.

They stopped at the base of the tree and there laid out on the ground was his tent and ground sheet. He was amazed to see all his space possessions being carried around and laid out each time exactly as he had done so meticulously the first night. His sense of humour kicked in and he thought that the Proto were almost 'taking the rise out of his ritual.' However, he though ruefully "if it made him – the visitor feel comfortable and happy, let the space visitor have his blanket and toys with him" as he prepared for sleep. Proto told Les to look up and to extend his inner lip, his tongue.

Les had learned by now that the floating 'pollen grains' which he adsorbed were the only nutrition he had, since meeting the Proto and he was also aware that he did not need to use the toilet or to drink water wherever it was. He still could find no trace of a water reservoir. He looked at his rations but they remained untouched.

Even his communicator and monitoring devices were up and supposedly running. He did not seem to care whether they were or not for some strange reason, it was not important at this time.

Anyhow after licking at the falling pollen grains, which fell from the top of the tree he was told by Proto to rest on his sheet. Les did feel as though he was tired and his eyes began to feel heavy. He wondered if the pollen was a drug or some narcotic, which brought on his sleepiness but they were on the move for a long time. He had lost all sense of time.

"Les..lie, the 'pollen' is food and it is good for Proto and you. It does not bring on sleep. By your time you have been awake for twelve hours of your day time. Proto must rest like you but we do not keep your time for rest and work. So you must rest for I must show you the night when we meet again. Proto must go to his family but he will always be close to you. Stop thinking so much Les..lie"

By the time Proto had finished his speech Les found himself laying into his usual foetal sleeping position and before he could answer, he could feel himself nod off.

METEORITES –
THE PERFECT TRANSPORT SYSTEM

Les work up suddenly, to the sound of some strange noise or call, which emanated from his dream. He could remember very little of his dreams which always seemed to be pleasant. He did his usual slit eyes routine and did not move until he scanned his surroundings. It looked as though it was still night time and he had no idea how long he had been asleep. He looked up and saw that he was lying on his sheet under the huge canopy of the great red Sequoia tree. He could see quite clearly through the trees so there was some light around as he was contemplating his solitude he felt much rested. He felt a slight buzz which was so fleeting that he could have just ignored it but he knew that he was been tuned into. He closed his eyes and reached out in his mind calling mentally to Proto, asking "Proto are you there?" A voice close to him said "why do you distrust Proto, Les..lie?," came the reply.

"Proto why do you ask such a question, I do not distrust you," replied Les.

"Then why do you awake and look around you before you open your eyes fully. It looks as though you feel that you will be hurt by some being" Proto continued.

Les was getting so used to telepathy so he just smiled to himself and said "Proto how could you know how I awaken myself?" he slyly replied knowing that he was found out.

"I know, Les...lie, because I have watched you every time you happen to be awakening" was the deliberate response.

At this Les sat up straight and stood up, looking around him rapidly. There right above him on a very tall branch was Proto sitting looking down at him with his bright big brown eyes flicking in a smiling way at him.

"Proto how long have you been here? Did you wake me with that buzz?" came the rapid confused questions as from someone who had prematurely awoken.

"Shhh ...," Proto, placed his mid digit to his slit mouth and his expressive eyes danced even more like the false eyes of the children's dolls of the twentieth century. Les had seen these dolls in the museum back on earth as a young lad. "Too many questions, I have been here all night. I thought that as it was close to night time again I wanted you to see the transporters in the sky. So yes I gave you a little nudge"

Les looked up at the smiling eyes of the figure, which remained perched over him suspended on the huge limb of the red tree. Proto looked so small at that great height. He smiled back and then Proto raised his spindly arm and pointed to him with the three fingers lined up tightly alongside each other. "Close your eyes, Les..lie."

Les did as he was told maintaining a fixed smile on his face. He felt his body sway and he knew that he was rising and he opened his eyes through slits only to see the ground being left under him as he rode up in an invisible elevator and in a few seconds he was sitting next to Proto, who folded his tiny arms. His eyes were even more expressive which gave the impression of a smiling person. Proto did not appear to have the muscles in his face even though his head was very large compared to the rest of his body. But this form of communication which is peculiar to humans was definitely present and could be felt by Les.

"Proto how do you move me so quickly and easily? Where do you get the power to lift and elevate up and down the trees?" inquired Les.

"Les..lie, you must be part of the whole life force. The mother tree gives us power to move to protect and to assist her with keeping the young Proto safe in the fields. Just as she made the wind to bring on fertilization or pollination so new Proto would be formed, she gives us the power to move around quickly and it is better to move through the air rather than walk. When Proto enter into the trees we are all connected and we meet our family immediately" was the simple reply. "Our mother tree controls all our movements, provides all food shelter and distributes the Proto as they are needed to work and to assist her with her plans, like I am helping her with you. Les..lie, you are my project !."

A pang of caution or warning passed through Les' mind. If he did not feel so protected and relaxed he would have become very suspicious and almost as reflex he asked Proto as they were both looking away in the distance through the huge branches, "What do you mean Proto, by saying that I am your project?."

Proto looked at him directly and for once the brown colour of his eyes were just slightly shimmering in the middle of his large white cornea and not dancing about, "I asked to be the one to show you who we were and to introduce Proto to your enquiries for we were all watching you." Proto continued, "You touched my hive first and we liked it when you touched it. All Proto also felt your touch. We know that you have a life task and so we must help you do that task since it concerns us. I asked to be the one to do the task for the hive. It was then granted by the mother tree that I should have the project, therefore you are my project."

Proto continued giving more information "Mother Tree causes the darkness to come, the pollen to feed us and allow us to become trees that hold all together. She also watches the Universe to see the different quadrants of the universe and when it is time to move our home or Planet and Sun from this area of the universe. She will move them to another part of the cosmos, by calling for help to others in the Universe.

Proto kept his eyes looking into the night sky and Les was fascinated looking at this new species which was telling him a 'child bed time story.' But all was said with none of the joy of storytelling or of fiction. Les knew that this new species which he just managed to meet was telling the truth to him as a matter of fact.

"Tonight you will see our Proto Translocator as it comes into the quadrant but first you and I will go down to the golden grass fields where we saw the new Proto added to the old unborn. However, I must show you some of the lifeless fertilization, very sad thing before we go down to the fields. In order to show it I must ask that you close your eyes as we travel, for it will be hard on your physique, Les..lie," he concluded. Les found that while he understood much of the religious life of Proto he felt that this being was relating the folk lore of his community. Being diplomatic, he decided that he will not indulge in any discussion of religious or biological philosophy. Indeed, he felt that he quite understood what the huge biological or rather botanical forms, were doing over the complete surface planet, and is what he had already known to happen in basic Botany.

It was advanced in that somehow the trees hid the zoological life forms within their insides. He was willing to believe what Proto had said that both the zoological and botanical forms of life on this very unusual planet may be inextricable bound together but then that also would be feasible. His biology knowledge was from his terran planet, Earth and it was an accepted fact that animals, birds and insects all work to the cycle of the flowering and fruiting of the plants. There were carnivores, which lived on the flesh of herbivores, so indirectly they also were dependent on the botanical forms of life.

For a fleeting moment Les realised that he was carrying out the information search of part of his mission. He looked over at Proto who was staring quietly into the night sky with unblinking eyes. He felt a great fondness for this creature which had asked to be his guide and who had taught him so much. He was about to make telepathic contact with Proto and called out but for some unknown reason he could not form thoughts in his head so he reached over to touch Proto to get his attention and for the first time in a long time tried to use his voice and a horrid croak came out. His eyes for once must have got to the size of Proto for he was struck that he was unable to use his voice. Proto turned and looked at him with a slight upward movement of his brown eyes and spoke out "Did you enjoy being yourself, Les..lie?."

Les felt the return of mental communication and with a shock asked, "Proto why did you break mental contact with me?"

The odd ungainly movement of the brown colour of his eyes returned when they appeared to be 'doll like' in movement and to be humorous. Proto replied matter of factly "It is necessary for you to have some privacy and not be part of our hive. When it is time for you to rejoin your family you will not have a problem with leaving us."

Les then wondered about how much control he really had of his thoughts of his planned duties and came to the conclusion that regardless of what he had to do on this mission and what his instructions were he was in fact doing the correct thing by being an ambassador to this odd and fascinating group of life forms. In all his studies of different life forms, found by earth scout and explorer space vessels, there were little humanoid forms ever encountered? At least those that were found were not intelligent forms capable of communication by any of the known forms to date with earth people. If only his instruments were recording all these wonderful conversations then surely ambassadors will follow up on his pioneer work.

With this thought Les turned to Proto with his biggest smile and said

> *"Your thoughtfulness is to be commended. You have the ability to read all my thoughts and even anticipate my questions before they are formed in my mind. You appear to have both the physical and spiritual power of all your natural surroundings at your command but you have chosen instead to give me an education about you and to share your knowledge with me so that I can bring it back to our peoples. Such behaviour is known to be the highest form of civilised behaviour. Thank you, Proto and the Mother Tree and the rest of your hive for your welcome to this space traveller"*

Les was pleased with this last speech to his alien friend for he was speaking as an ambassador for all earth people. The history of earth's population involved with space exploration is filled with wonderful speeches given by those pioneers, who did the first act or found the first important relic, or made other findings, which fitted into the grand plan designed by much more important and cleverer folks than those actually doing the job. Les thought that he was just an ordinary man doing the science which he loved but in the broader expanse of space. He thought of himself as a kind and understanding man. He also felt that his attributes of not feeling too strongly about most things based on his private philosophy that everyone is entitled to his/her opinion allowed most of the more assertive people to convince others of whatever they are saying. In his case by his quiet demeanour and non combative attitude as well as, his attention to the individual making a forceful point gave confidence to the protagonist. This of course made him sort of popular since he was considered to be a 'nice bloke' to have around. In actual fact he was just thought to be inoffensive. Many knew that he was quite clever at whatever science he was doing but no one really knew other that his closest superiors. He was rarely given the opportunity to talk about his work to anyone since he was always the one listening.

His thoughtful rambling were made to some extent to justify why he was the chosen one. This was an unusual position for Les to be in but then he thought that it had all begun by being chosen to come on this mission at the start. Afterall his discipline, dealing with the microbes in space, was really one of the most innocuous of all the disciplines. In fact, to use the idiom of an earlier time on earth's planet, it was not a 'very sexy' subject and only merited any attention when there was an infectious disease problem. Few of the really brilliant graduates of the Academy ever showed any interest in the subject, other than to make a good grade in the early part of their training so they could go forward on the really 'sexy professions' such as Astrophysics or Cosmo-exobiology, which essentially dealt with the use of technology to manipulate DNA in a space environment. The main reason was that it was possible to get results in a faster time frame than would be possible, if such experiments were done on earth or in the presence of any gravitational atmosphere. As a result, there were rich rewards and more patents filed in that discipline than any of the other sciences.

In his world he was driven by the rewards of financial security and movement up the administrative ladder, within the Space Exploration Agency. This was one of, if not the most powerful and important Corporation, on Earth. This was the goal of many of the students at the Academy, who felt the need to repay their parents in prestige, who supported them throughout their academic training. Essentially, Microbiologists were only needed to solve the problem as to why an infectious problem began in the first place. This role evolved later on because scientists could use the ability of microbes to experiment with genetically, thus solving many human infectious problems. Much of this was accomplished over two hundred years ago on Earth. It was then thought that there would be a wonderful opportunity to develop the discipline in space research, where 'new microbes' could be exploited to continue development that would be beneficial to earthlings. While this was exciting to begin with, the enthusiasm and support soon petered out because the biochemists developed automated systems which detected the products of microbial respiration and enzymic digestion of complex proteins and carbohydrates. The need for the pure Microbiologist also diminished.

Les yawned then felt Proto touch his arm. "Les..lie, it is time to communicate with Proto. We must go higher up to see the undeveloped Proto and await the passing of the meteors in the sky – it is The Coming." Les felt the need to ask what 'The Coming' meant but he knew that all would be explained in time. So he asked Proto, "How often does 'The Coming' appear to the Proto?"

Proto was standing and turned to look at Les, with a serious, intent direct eye to eye contact fixed on Les' question and after a time, he slowly responded, "The last time was over one thousand years ago in your time. Proto and his hive were not there at that time but his earlier family, who were chosen, is still on the golden plains."

He continued "While Proto live for a long time our Mother Tree know that we must rest, so some Proto volunteer after five to six hundred years to become seeds which form new Proto. Others live to be over two to three thousand years old." Proto extended his digit to Les, who automatically held out his hand to clasp the three digits and closed his eyes. The sensation was imperceptible but by now he could feel the slight movement upwards. He tried to slit his eyes and found that he could and glancing at Proto, who had his neck and head looking upwards, he noticed Proto's other hand was brushing the main trunk but only lightly and it was obvious that the power or force for this movement came from this beautiful, massive red tree.

The upper canopy of this Mother Tree appeared to be younger and healthier as they rose upwards. Les scanned these upper branches, which still appeared to be young and growing and to be swaying in the breeze. They arrived at another lateral branch which allowed visibility at its end to reveal the night sky. It was a dark intense blue rather than a black sky and he could see many star formations but all were unknown to him.

By some mystical light he could see a number of small meteors, more like large rocks passing away in the distance. It was if Les was looking through the port hole of the mother space ship which had brought him and the crew to explore this segment of space.

Again Proto touched his arm and communicated, "Les..lie, you will enter the Mother Tree to see the unborn undeveloped Proto. Hold my digits close to your chest and walk with me to the centre where the branch where we are standing touches the main trunk of the Mother Tree." Les did as he was asked to do and like two dancers facing each other they did a 'crab-like' walk towards the middle of the tree.

The trunk of the Mother Tree had a huge knot facing them. Proto touched the middle of the knot, which immediately opened and Les found that he was no longer touching Proto's digits but that he was standing in a huge living room type of setting. There was a pale light which emanated from the walls within the opening through which they had just entered. The opening closed immediately after their entry. Proto was on his knees and his head was bent in some sort of supplication. Les followed automatically and also bowed his head but he went further and placed both the palms of his hands together as though praying. Some of the earth people still do so in some of the quiet corners of Earth. This action by Les brought a small shiver to the whole tree, which was like a tiny earth quake commonly felt on earth. Les kept his eyes closed and slightly shifted his weight on his knees to compensate for the movement of the tree which was short lived.

There was a slight ringing in his ears, which was very pleasant then a thin female-like voice sang out, "Les..lie you have impeccable manners. Proto was right to ask for you as a project. You have learned much and yes to your question, we do have some imperfections. Feel with your mind as I open up the next chamber for you to see." Les felt an intense happiness as the voice sang out in his mind. He could see another bed chamber as if it was from an old historical earth movie. There was a yellow glow and in it were several of the "fruit like oval marble like forms" about the size of three to four feet in diameter. He could feel them as hard. He could also see Proto reach out and touch one of them but with the odd digit. There was a bright flash as it immediately split evenly into two halves. A pink glow emanated from inside. He mentally saw himself move to look at the halves and he saw a small Proto lying as though fast asleep inside but coiled in a foetal position. It looked like the inside of a cradle. Then Proto pointed to the feet but they were not separated but appeared joined together like a tear shaped leaf. Then the singing voice said, "This Proto will be absorbed to be food for Me the Mother Tree. A newly formed Proto will be made some time in the future."

Les was astonished at what he had seen and he could still feel his hands clasped in the praying position. He knew that he had been paid one of the best compliments ever that one race or species can ever give to another. A slight breeze caressed his face and almost imperceptibly he found himself standing on the outside branch through which Proto and he had just entered. Proto was looking at him with those dancing brown eyes. He reached out and embraced this thin little lithe figure and felt his arms meeting together at the back. He then realised how physically fragile his friend Proto really was.

Proto appeared to be taken by the surprise hug from Les and his eyes moved rapidly almost frantically but Les knew that Proto was overwhelmingly happy for this was forced into Les' mind. Suddenly, there was an extreme brightness penetrating the branches of the canopy of the entire tree and the surrounding area beyond the cover of the tree. The golden grass shone brighter and yellower than ever, indeed the whole sight looked like the painting of one of the wheat fields which he had seen in one of the art gallery museums back on earth. Proto pointed upwards towards the night sky which was also as clear and bright as daylight. Like a ball of yellow to white light came a meteor high up above with a long tail dragging behind but shedding an uncanny light around the whole land area. It arched in the sky some many million miles out in space but its light intensity was too great relative to the small sight in the distance. Just as quickly it disappeared and there was an even more intense darkness.

All the bedtime children ramblings of Proto were explained in an instant to Les and he could feel an excitement in the air. His guide and protector looked at him and extended his three digits for Les to hold onto as he also automatically closed his eyes. He felt a lifting of his body but this time he did not feel the urge to open his eyes. There was a constant breeze passing his whole body and it was some time before he felt the light touch of the ground under his feet. Proto's digits did not remove readily and Les did not open his eyes immediately for he sensed that something extraordinary was about to happen.

After what appeared to be about five minutes, in reality it was just about thirty seconds, of his time, he felt the slow melting away of Proto's digits. Les found that they were standing at the edge of the large grassy plains in twilight. They had covered a distance of over ten to fifteen kilometres in just a few minutes. .He was completely taken back by the tremendous activity which was taking place and all very silently. In the time he was with Proto, he was aware of a number of other Proto around. He did see quite a few as the fruiting spores were being rolled into the grassy plains but now they were crowded over by hundreds of moving figures all of whom were Proto-like forms.

Proto touched him and they were elevated to about the same height as the day before approximately fifty feet when he witnessed the harvesting task done by a collective farming community. It was reminiscent of the early nineteen or twentieth century farming practise back on earth, with one difference for this farming of was done by alien life forms. From this elevated vantage point Les, could see for the first time the great area of the massive grass field with its yellow to gold surreal reflected light. He also saw hundreds or thousands of Proto moving towards the perimeter of the field. "Les..lie, we are in the hundreds of thousands of Proto, near enough to a million of your citizens," volunteered Proto. Les turned to look at Proto who was looking at him intently and obviously read or anticipated his question as to their numbers on the planet. All these living animal bi pedal forms of life and none of the sensors picked up any evidence of life forms – similar to that of a primate species. Then an almost hopeless thought crossed his mind as to just how effective is the technology used by us earthlings. No evidence of any living animal form of life while there are literally a million or several millions all secretly watching them land and bring their helpless technology with them. This was an incongruity which had to be explained.

Before he could ask why so many Proto were around at this time of night and what they were doing. Proto lowered them back to the ground. Again he gave a pre-emptive answer in his simple telepathic monotone, "Les..lie, I shall have to leave you for awhile. I will come back to you after I have contributed to the hive. You will be placed onto the nearest branch of the mother tree to see what few of us Proto have ever seen other than those who are over one thousand years old or more. There are very few since most Proto prefer to give themselves up to form new Proto.

Again Les felt as though Proto was showing the ability to read his thoughts as they are formed but at times Les thought that he was capable of reading those thoughts before Les had formulated them. Proto reached out for his hand and as a reflex, Les closed his eyes and within seconds he was sitting on a branch which was as wide as fifteen feet and he was just sitting crossed legged on the surface. When he looked straight ahead he could see the massive expanse of the savannah plain several hundred miles square all filled with the continuous swaying of the large golden grass leaves.

He now noticed there was the continual bobbing of heads with many appearing like tiny stick figures with square heads. Proto kept looking at the scene anxiously and Les got the impression that he wanted to join that mass out in the plain. Before he could give his approval, Proto broke into his thoughts and said "Thanks, Leslie. I shall be back as soon as we have finished our task. The Proto are ready to be released for the Mother Tree has been collecting the unborn for many thousands of years." Les watched as Proto walked away from him and straight into the main trunk of the Mother tree and simply disappeared. He turned his eyes at the scene below and in front of him. The silence was deafening and his mind appeared to be empty of any thoughts. He then began to think of the mundane and how could so many sentient beings collect themselves in the field below without betraying any sound. It was as if they were all responding to telepathic instructions but he was not able to connect with any Proto. Ha! He thought to himself, they are using another wave length or bandwidth which is leaving me out of the loop and he laughed to himself.

It was interesting to note that there was some diversity in the colour of the Proto skin and in their eye colour. Why Les thought of this seemingly useless piece of information could not be explained. In his reverie and in the silence Les noted that there was a change in the activity for all the Proto were lined up around the perimeter of the field of golden grass. The wind which was causing the grass fronds to wave had stopped.

Then as if by some uncanny form of military instruction, all the Proto bowed their box-like heads and it was an odd site. Les again felt a little shudder taking place on the big Sequoia or Mother Tree but it was almost imperceptible.

Almost immediately a wind erupted on the grassy plain and there was a swishing sound as the grass blades swung against each other. Soon this wind developed into a localised while-wind storm which appeared very odd from his perch high in the Sequoia tree. There was still no effect on the Mother Tree but Les now heard the noise of the wind rustling in the grass leading up to the huge red tree. While the noise was still very low it was noticeable and rising. Dust from the round began to rise into the air and from his perch Les could see and hear the powerful force of the wind on the plains as it bent the tall golden grasses to the ground. The incongruous part, was while all this atmospheric upheaval was building up, the Proto remained silent on the perimeter of the large field with their heads still bent.

Then the 'penny dropped' for Les, who now realised with some shock and surprise that the wind was being caused by the collective 'Hive of Proto' who were combining their will and mental strength to cause the formation of an old fashion tornado funnel. This whole process was developing right in front of him and for the first time in a long time Les could feel the force and intensity increase to a terrifying level. Although he felt safe on his perch, even in the Mother Tree the power could be felt on the ground supporting this magnificent tree so even it began to tremble slightly. He stood up as if to get a better view but he was already having the best view. It was just that he was caught up with the excitement at looking at a change in weather taking place around him but he was in a zone of utter calm. This pastoral scene with its picturesque forest of magnificent forests where he has been living and enjoying every moment of his time there was showing the signs of a catastrophe about to happen.

From the plain a humming sound began to grow louder. Les thought that the sound was coming from the line of Proto surrounding the plain but he could follow the notes, which appear to be coming from the upper branches of his tree, 'The Mother Tree.' The humming changed key and sounded like a lullaby soft lilting and cooing. It soon became louder than the sound of the stormy wind blowing around and across the grass lands.

Les felt a peaceful calm overtake him and he settled down into a sitting position facing the spectacle in front of him. He then noted a movement across the grassy plains which he thought at first was the wind blowing across the surface of the now flattened grasses. He continued to look across the fields and these wisps of movement built up like a torrent of rivulets all moving into the centre of the plain. As the crescendo of the lullaby increased the rivulets of little rapid moving forms was revealed to be the round hardened globes which were strewn on the plain of golden grasses. He thought that he had seen a few hundreds, maybe at most a few thousands. What he was witnessing was a torrent of these hardened egg or spores containing foetal Proto all heading or being pushed by the force of a 'hurricane-like' low lying wind into the centre of the field.

There had to be many hundreds of thousands moving at rapid speed of over three hundred kilometres per hour. As the first mass of these spore-like forms reached the centre, almost instantly the heads of the Proto on the circumference of the field began to rise slowly and the mass of spores also began to form a pillar. Because of their now pale brown to whitish colour it looked like an old fashioned Grecian Doric Column. The as more were added to the poll in the centre location, the mass began to tower until it looked like it was going to get to his level which was over four hundred feet high. Les was mesmerised by the sight as the number of spores were added so furiously and with such large numbers that the level of the tower rapidly passed his level and shot up higher than the Mother Tree.

The golden grasses on the plains began to lose their shimmer and the field was darkening except for the glow given off by the wind directed spore tower. The sound of the wind was jarring to Les' ear drums which were unaccustomed to erratic noises for such a long time. He placed his hands over his ears but now there was the intense lullaby which was bringing calm around the column. The column of eggs was moving with a centrifugal force of such power, speed and focussed direction that the individual round spores could not be detected.

Les was looking at this show of absolute power and control and when he did move his eyes from the magnificent tower, he could see the Proto clearly with their heads fully tilted towards the night sky. For the first time, Les felt the great tree breathing like a huge pump as its branches began to shiver. Suddenly, with a loud ear splitting scream from the heavens, an intense light filled the whole field including the continuous covered canopy. Les tried to look upwards but the intensity of the light was too bright so he turned his eyes towards the ground. There he could see the base of the tower of Proto containing spores begin to shimmer like a golden pillar reflecting on the surrounding field a golden colour and brightness as in broad daylight.

All this was followed by a phenomenally increasing level of sound. This made him squeeze the palms of his hands to his ears even tighter, while looking away from the bright light above. Les thought that his mother space ship was about to crash but of course his ship was nowhere close to this planet.

Just as he thought that his ear drums would burst, he saw the pillar of golden spinning spores lift off the ground and shoot upwards out of the surface of the planet. As he watched transfixed in awe, the column of tightly packed Proto spores shot off into space with a speed unlike anything he had ever heard or witnessed in his whole life. He could not help but continue to look at this now departing bright tower of spores, when a rapidly moving comet with a bright tail came into view and appeared to be on a collision course with the massive tower of spores. As the two forces met, there was a blink in the combined light's intensity but both seemed to merge into each other. It was obvious that the pillar of Proto containing spores, was heading out of this quadrant of space and deeper into outer space. All this was too much for Les, who closed his eyes and slid onto the floor of the branch where he was watching the spectacle, on the huge Mother Tree. He lost consciousness.

SPEAK NO EVIL.

Les awoke from his sleeping or *fainting spell* unaware of how long he was not conscious. He looked around him only to see a concerned Proto sitting and staring down at him. They were on his bed roll on the ground at the edge of the forest where he had spent the first night. As he looked around him he saw the carefully laid out monitoring and camp surrounding equipment just as he had done that first night when he had entered this remarkable forest. He quickly recalled the events before he had spoken for he realised how close and protected he was by his alien friend of the past two or three weeks. The smooth bark of his pillow tree was at his back.

He sat up and found that his head was quite clear. Indeed, he had a special feeling of overwhelming happiness and of goodwill to everyone and all things around him. He looked especially at the concerned face of Proto, whose face and small features he had sub consciously learned to interpret despite the enigmatic appearance of his almost dour demeanour. He smiled broadly and said, "Hello Proto my little magician friend. How long have I laid here?" as he stood up and looked around and down at Proto.

Proto asked quietly again the telepathic communication was so easy for them both to use."Are you alright, Les..lie? You have been asleep for a very long time and I was worried that you became too stressed by our 're-seeding of the universe ritual."Mother Tree said that you appeared to be enjoying yourself but when I returned back to you I found that you were in a deep sleep and I was told not to awake but to let you recover on your own, Les..lie"

Proto paused and Les spoke up "well, how long have I been asleep, Proto?" he inquired reluctantly knowing that it must have been for a long time.

"Four of your twenty four hours" came the droll reply. "Four days!" exclaimed Les "You mean that I have been out of it for four days. "Wow! I feel fine I mean wonderful. You and your hive put on a wonderful display. I have never seen or heard of any such thing in my life before. I just could not believe that the mental power of your combined hive was so great as to send all your brethren to join that comet. I just do not understand why after accumulating so many unborn Proto you just blasted them out into space?"

Proto listened then quietly asked, "Do you not understand how we have used the 'comet' to take our new Proto throughout the Universe?"

Proto continued, "We call the comet the Proto Translocator. It carries the unborn Proto throughout the universe until it finds a planet, which has all the right conditions then it releases the Proto like small meteorites onto the surface. Within a number of years new Proto will be formed and will be just like us." Proto looked at Les with his dancing eyes then continued: "A Mother Tree will develop and she will give life to all that is needed on the new planet. The cycle will develop and another Proto Translocator will be called upon to carry another Hive away into the cosmos. That is the mission of all the Proto."

Proto remained silent as Les looked intently at him. "Proto I must ask this of you and I apologise in advance "but are you Proto, planning to conquer the Universe?" Les knew that this was a very insolent question to ask of his friend but he knew that he would get an honest reply. "But of course, Les..lie. But I would not say conquer. We have no flight machines like you and your species. We do not have a military body which plans to take over other civilizations"

"Les..lie, we create new conditions for civilizations to develop. We make the new planets habitable for new forms of life to develop as the planet conditions require them. We are the Proto. From us Proto – Les.. lie: all life develops. We are the first, we are the Proto."

He continued, "Our secret to you is that YOU, Les..lie, were also developed from Proto many long centuries ago. Our Mother Tree said that this was the first time that a life form has returned and it was exciting for her to be the one to welcome back an evolved species from one of the Proto several millions of your years ago. You, Earthlings are the offspring of an ancient Proto."

There was a slight pause as his alien friend continued "Proto will never show ourselves again to any of its future life forms in any part of the Universe, even in the expanses which are being created billions of your light years away. We shall be going there after you leave us"

Les found himself sitting near to Proto who was speaking in a casual manner on this most profound of subject. His mind was vivid and he was taking in the significance of what is being said to him. He knew for the first time he was being lectured to in the best possible manner and his insignificance in the cosmos caused his shoulders to sag under the weight of what was being said to him. On the other hand why was he the privileged one to find out the origin of Man.? If what he just heard is true and he had no reason to disbelieve this being sitting in front of him looking intently at him with no movement of his brown eyes.

"Proto I do not understand how we could have evolved from you, we are so different physically and we do not have your telepathic power or your skill of kinetic self transportation or ability to levitate. We cannot enter into trees or become trees or anything else for that matter. For the first time Les thought he heard a physical laughter sound coming from his slim fragile companion and looked up to see the shy dancing eyes appear as well, there was a slight opening of the slit mouth but showing no teeth or anything else. "Les..lie, but you are made of the same substance as your surroundings on your planet Earth. In the early history of your evolution and in some of your 'races' the ability to levitate, and to 'thought travel' were common. Your species did lose some of that ability. Instinctively, you have always protected the trees. You have even farmed the trees, which were your life source. Why do you think that you did that? Your science did work out how the evolved forms of the 'animal life forms' and plant life are interdependent. What you lost was the ability to become one with the plants. But it was not important for you to remain as Proto for you had to evolve differently since diversity was needed to maintain the life forms in your part of the cosmos or galaxy"

Les was pensive, with an absolutely blank mind, he asked Proto "When will I meet my colleagues. I have lost all concepts of time and space."

"You will meet them now, Les..lie. Please close your eyes and count to three as a digit moved and touched his hand." He laughed to himself and counted in his mind to three. He opened his eyes and there he was standing just out of site of the explorer at the edge of the forest. He heard laughter coming from the shuttle, which was showing some of the light from within.

It was early evening. He looked at the brown laughing eyes of Proto, who appeared to be happy. Les was happy and he placed a hand around the shoulder of Proto, whose eyes danced so rapidly and the slit mouth remained ajar for a long time. He however, felt a surge of power running through his body which caused him to shiver. The skin of Proto was so smooth and warm against his bare forearm. At the same time, he found that he was grinning broadly. He knew automatically that he was the only one who had this experience and he knew that Proto would not show himself to the others. He also had a feeling that he accomplished a great deal and that his task was completed. Proto pointed to his shuttle then said, "You will only remember some of what you have seen. The rest will come to you bit by bit and the rest later when you are very old. I have a gift for you, Les..lie."

Proto stooped down and picked up a white stone about the size of his thumbs lying by his side and handed them to Les. He slipped the flat stones into his pocket. He looked up to Proto and said "I must go now. Good bye my friend and tutor," and he held up one hand in a parting salutation. He turned his back and began down the shallow hill. Halfway down, he turned around and he saw, Proto with his hands upwards. Before his eyes a large spruce tree took root. He looked back as a huge spruce tree rose up to over twenty feet tall. He knew that it was not there. He continued towards the laughter coming from the shuttle.

REUNION

"Hello there! Just in time for we have only just arrived" said the laughing Tara, whom he had never seen laugh so broadly or enthusiastically before. They both approached him with such great joy, welcoming and threw their arms around him. This familiarity was not present before, in fact it was not present among any of the crew at least, none of the crew that he knew. He loved this reunion. They were all trying to speak at the same time including him. They soon settled down. Little did Les know that they were placed into a state of deep sleep and happiness by the Proto for only he was chosen as a witness and he would never know why as long as he lived.

Tara spoke first and said that she could find no water on the surface but believes from the lushness of the vegetation that there must be very deep aquifers under the rocks. She did collect some samples but they appeared to be withering away. She had collected some pollen but they were so small. She said that she enjoyed sticking out her tongue to collect them. Then they all said that they had done the same thing. It looks as though they were behaving just like students at University for they broke out into hilarious laughter. Les said that his trip was a total failure for he could not collect or detect any of the acceptable or well known minerals. There were traces of Na, K with minute traces of C and S. It was the most insignificant findings anyone could have stumbled amongst this planet of so much vegetation. His geologic findings did not reveal a hot centre and there were no volcanoes. Tara interrupted and said that she had found a combination of Carbon, Hydrogen, Oxygen and Nitrogen in such a combination that photosynthesis, under the broader light bands of ultra violet light and infra red part of the spectrum coming from the sun revealed that the chlorophyll of the tress were functioning at near enough one hundred percent efficiency. She felt that the specialist botanists from the mother ship may want to have a more in depth look at the planet. However, she had collected some samples and had video recorded as much as was possible with her equipment. She did note that she had collected some leaves at evening before she turned in and she could not help but notice that they had disappeared the next morning.

Everyone appeared to be healthy and in good and positive spirits. They noted that they had hardly used any of their rations and when they collaborated with each other they just broke out laughing again. They all felt super healthy and they had no explanation for their obvious vigour and almost cavalier attitude to this their first mission. After a good night's rest they woke up almost simultaneously and began preparations for departure. They had all their equipment and sleeping gear which they had taken with them. They had plugged themselves into their computers to download their findings. It also recorded their physical health and mental aptitude. If anything they all appeared to be healthier than when they had left the shuttle.

It was a smooth and almost dull return home with absolutely no problems other than the fact that they were in such an ebullient mood. As they approached the mother ship, they were contacted and shown a port along the side where they were to enter. The mother ship which they had not seen for such a long time, seemed to be just waiting for them. It lay like a huge suckling pig showing the port entrances which looked like her teats. They noticed the number of explorer shuttles which were docking and leaving their stations that the information collectors must have been over worked. They were working twenty four hours continuously.

Tara was the first to be debriefed as the Leader of the team. She also transferred all the data and video data from the shuttle computer which they controlled. There were computers on the shuttle which stored data involuntarily and operated independently of the crew. Tara had to explain the obvious lack of surface water in this lush planet. The odd occurrence was when Tara was told that the long range scans of the Mother Ship could not locate either the sun or planet in that quadrant from which they had just explored for the past three to four weeks. This was none of her responsibilities and in a short while after telling her other two fellow crew members; they soon forgot all that they had experienced. The medical review showed that for some reason the genetic high blood pressure which was a permanent document on Les health record had been changed. It no longer was detectable. So also were some of the transient illnesses on the other partners of this trip. Even old broken bones could not be detected.

Nolo Contendere

Les went up to the observation deck of the mother ship to look out at the passing shuttles but also to scan the surrounding stars in this galaxy. There was no argument that he could bring into his mind for he may have also been duped by the hallucinogen pollen on the planet. As he was standing there by himself he tucked his hands into his pocket, which were normally empty. He felt a hard smooth form and pulled out the shiny white almost marble like pebble, which was given to him by Proto just before he went into the shuttle to join the others.

He had kept much of his experiences away from the others. He looked at the oval form in his hand and felt it begin to glow white and become warm. He cupped it in his closed hands to see the white glow intensify in the shallow darkness of his hands. He brought it up closer to his eyes and for a fleeting moment it became warmer, then translucent. A small face with dancing, smiling eyes appeared, winked and disappeared. He looked shocked as the pebble became a dull white form in his hands. He stuck it back into his pocket.

The End

SPACE ACADEMY

(written more than twenty years ago
to entertain my two girl children)

INTRODUCTION

Humans have spent a fortune setting up listening outposts in
the cosmos, seeking sentient forms of life. Maybe such alien
beings are already here. They have been taking away individuals,
educating them and re releasing them into society. This speeds up
human evolution through intellectuals in earth's population.

THE FAMILY

It was early summer and like all the suburban families in the subdivision everyone sleeps in on Saturday morning. It was no different for Don and Donna Mills. They were Laboratory Scientists and they were "On Call" for the laboratories shift this weekend, so they enjoyed a 'lay in' at least until the telephone rang for their services.

Don and Donna had moved to a new city to live and it was no coincidence that the name of the city was London. As well, they had brought their first house and had the time to begin a family which eventually was made of two daughters.

They have often discussed how lucky they were to have taken such a chance and how fortunate they were to have met such wonderful folks who rapidly became their friends. In fact they had both thought out their future plans very well for they had both achieved what they had originally wanted to do.

Then it was that fatal evening as Don used to call it when Donna said to him "well, should we begin to think of having a family or not? I am getting into my thirties and it is not healthy to begin having children in my thirties"

Don said that he had not thought too much a family, since he had come from a relatively large family while Donna was an only child. Both her parents had passed away when she was just turning twenty. First was her Mum and when she was twenty three her dad also succumbed to cancer. She had carried on with her studies and her internship until she had her first advanced diploma.

She knew that Don was ambivalent about having any children, since he remembered his own childhood when there were none of the joys in belonging to a large family, as depicted in the movies of the fifties. The world in which they found themselves was new in so many ways so they quickly gave up much of the "old baggage" which they had brought with them from the old country. They embraced the new foods, the music and the pseudo-academic way of living. Their friends appeared to give them the benefit of their back ground, as though they were extra clever, since they had come from 'jolly old England'. They both began to become leaders in their respective jobs and over time had built a reputation of some 'upper class' practices. While harmless, they were not arrogant but rather discouraged others from taking life too seriously.

So it was that after much discussion with their group of friends, which were made up of a wide range of ages. They cautiously made prudent enquiries from those who did not have any children and found out that if those folks had to do it all over again, they would have a family. They had both done quite a bit of travelling to the West Indies and to Europe and had settled down in their professions. There were not very much more that they really wanted to accomplish outside of their jobs. And like everything that this immigrant family did they approached having a family just as cautiously.

Donna came off the pill for the required amount of time specified by her obstetrician. Support came from Don, even when he had to put up with the complications of not just rolling over for sex but actually having to prepare to have intercourse by using condoms and creams et cetera. They had their laugh and within three years they had two lovely daughters separated by two years. They just could not swing the one boy one girl part to make it perfect. With no immediate family in the country, they began taking trips to show their offspring to Donna's cousin's aunts and uncles in England. They knew that they were lucky to have such beautiful kids and of course, they had to take the children to Don's mother and father, who were also ecstatic. It appears that all was well.

After each pregnancy, Donna and Don were lucky to find a surrogate 'Grandma' as a baby sitter within the sub division. This was a remarkable person who had just moved into their area after she and her husband had sold off their farm in Western Ontario to retire in the suburbia of the city of London. They were successful in raising six children of their own and many of whom were working in the southwest area. This unusual baby sitter did everything they had said that they wanted her to do, for the children. When Don and Donna came home from work, both children were showered dressed up in their pretty clothing and were well fed. It was a dream, come true for this hard working couple. Don and Donna had read that the children should be exposed to music as small babies so they took out a selection of classical music and showed "Grandma" how to put on the player so she could play the music quietly as the babies had their afternoon nap.

When the children were old enough to have stories read to them, there were lots of books around as well as stories on records. Indeed the black and white television, which sat on a small table in the corner of the room, was rarely on except for a sport game or for the news. The CBC Radio was almost their sole source of home entertainment along with their now vast collection of records, hundreds of novels and hard cover first publications of their favourite authors. Life was organized and in full bloom for the Mills family. They continued to attend the summer theatre, musicals and classical recitals with a now select number of friends. Because of the size of this country, it was to be expected that many of their colleagues and friends would move for better opportunities of employment or for family reasons.

A discussion as to how to educate their children came up one evening, when there was a lovely supper and much wine followed by the usual after supper brandy and liqueurs. They always had wonderful friends who brought up great topics of discussions, which were lively interesting but most of all informative. Here was a topic, which Don and Donna were aware that they had to deal with, in the next year or two since the older of their children Elizabeth, was going to be three years at her next birthday. Their second daughter was having her first birthday. The family only had advanced education in their new own country and did not know anything about the schooling system in Canada at the kindergarten, primary school or the high school level. What opinions that they did have, were not very good, since the bad news was often what was heard and not the successes.

Their friends were also at a loss to give worthwhile opinions since many were born outside the country and had to retrain, while others never took a Canadian diploma since they felt that their training in Europe was far superior to anything this country had to offer in the 1960's to 1970's. Both Don and Donna did not agree with this type of attitude or with such back handed comments. .After one of those husband and wife quiet discussions, it was Don who remarked "you know Donna, I do not understand some of our European friends who still run down this new country of ours" Donna looked up from her cross word which was on her lap placed the newspaper page on the coffee table and replied "I agree, we have embraced this new country totally and we do not intend to ever go back to Europe or any other part of the world to live for that matter" However, there were colleagues and friends who were born in Canada or came as very young children from other countries and of course they felt differently as well.

The offspring of these first generation immigrants were brought up under the Canadian Education system and were citizens *extra ordinaire*. Don continued his thoughtful conversation "you know as a lecturer in this country Donna. the Canadian system is a modern one and provides a wide range of choices in the various subjects. In the UK they had a fixed number of subjects with little or no choice ot broaden one's view on other subjects of interest" There was silence for they knew that while some of the less progressive students chose the quick way out they then became the low wage earners having non progressive positions. There are the others who because of upbringing or driven by ambitious parents and family cause the children to work and be more academically ambitious at school. Those were the ones who did not avoid the difficult subjects. Indeed, they may have even sought out the challenges of the more difficult subjects. Of course, that was where the opportunities existed. As a result these graduates by choice were hired by the growth in technology companies. This meant better pay for the companies also invested in their success.

It was after an evening of wine food and healthy conversation with a Canadian couple who had no children that the debate over what to do about the children's initial schooling took place. Dona and Donna made the decision to begin the process of their children's educational course by sending them to the Montessori Private School System. While this was a well developed system in Europe it was just catching on in the city of London. They both thought that the good thing about this was that the girls began school at just under three years of age for Elizabeth and Ellen two years younger was also initiated a little earlier.

Don and Donna were very pleased with the girls progress and in those early days both children could read many of the children books by the time they were three years old. They also developed a passion for all things which required reading writing and sums or arithmetic. It was a treat to have them chat about their achievements at supper time and encouragement from their parents just enhanced their progress. Both parents although they tried to down play the children's progress at social occasions still could not help but be proud about how their little girls were progressing.

This story begins at this stage of the children's education as both parents became enthusiastic about educating their daughters. They were willing to sacrifice almost anything to let their little girls get the best education going. After education was the key to their modicum of success so it must also be good for their progeny.

AFTER A NIGHT OF FOOD, WINE AND COMPANY

"Donna, what time is it, luv" Don asked as they slowly became awake. Donna also yawned making herself awake and reached over to pick Don's watch from the bedside table. She always transferred Don's watch every night from his bedside table to her right side night table next to her glass of water. This little idiosyncrasy had become a ritual for more than ten years. His watch was always twenty to thirty minutes late and it had been so for many months. Don said to himself that he must get his watch fixed but he just never got around to doing anything about his dysfunctional watch. They had both become accustomed to adjusting their routine to take in the extra minutes.

"It is seven a.m., and it is Saturday so go back to sleep. You do not have to go into the hospital laboratory today and you are not 'On Call'"

"That's right" Don responded as he yawned again."Thought I heard the girls' voices, are they up as yet?" he asked sleepily.

"No, turn over and I will give you a cuddle," she replied.

"OK" and turned his back to Donna. "What did we do last evening?" he yawned again. But Don did not feel like going back to sleep and so he lay quietly as Donna placed her arms around his chest and began to snore.

Whenever he became awake he began to think of the past week and this was no different. He thought to himself: *what a week he had, with the plans to open the new laboratory or rather the refurbished laboratory quarters. It was the same space and location but the contractors had done a good job rebuilding the space into more modern quarters. It now included all the regulatory and mandated precautions for a safe work place, thanks to the unions and the Government Regulations. The health of the working staff, which included the professional medical technologists, was now given a priority since they were always dealing with potentially infectious specimens from sick patients. But all did not go well over the last few weeks for he knew changes were made by the Old Medical Director, who took over from him while he was on vacation. Of course, it was Murphy's Law if anything had to go wrong it would be at the time he was away and the old Brit thought that he knew everything and so made decisions to alter some parts of the plans. For Don, this was a nightmare since he had to have administrative support for any changes to realign any of the contractual alterations.*

He also thought that it was a jolly good thing that he had taken the time to check out his lab space for he found a Mirror and soap dispenser on the wall but there was no sink or water outlet on the wall.

He thought loudly to himself, "What do these workmen think about" He became arrogant, thinking that the workmen found his assumption to begin with was wrong. The administration tended to take the workmen's suggestion over his and laughed to himself at the thought of workers capable of independent thought. These early meanderings of thought revealed that work of the past week was still on his mind. But his thoughts became more passive as he made himself awake." Crickey Man! One would think as the guy was putting up the mirror and a soap dish, he might just mention to the foreman that this was odd and ask shouldn't a sink go with this assembly?" This work crew worked as though they were robots. The plans did call for a Wall Cabinet and he wondered maybe the chap could not read. He might have been one of those new immigrant workers, who could not read. But this was nonsense since the trades were full of immigrant workers, who were trained in their respective country. They may not be able to read but they certainly knew their craft more so than the young 'Turks' who leave school prematurely and feel that they can make big bucks in the building industry, which appears to take them on without any interview.

He did not really pick on the immigrants since he was very conscious that he was an immigrant and has been in Canada for more than fourteen years. He came to this conclusion as he rolled over onto his back fully awake and he could hear Donna breathing regularly next to him. She had gone back to sleep. My goodness he thought to himself fourteen years and they never thought once of leaving to go elsewhere in Canada. There were job offerings and he remembered when a colleague called to ask him if he wanted to take her position in Vancouver, actually on the island. At that time he was having a bit of a rough time with the old Brit in charge of Laboratory Medicine.

He went off for the interview and who did he happen to meet but a younger Brit from the North Country, who felt that he was in the colonies and his job was that of the "Raj in her Majesty's Service." When he thought of the salary and the offer of this man with a thick Lancashire accent, who also offered to pay his moving expenses, it was a plum position. His main reason for moving from Ontario was the persecution by another older Brit. He would be jumping from the frying pan into the fire. No thank you and after discussion with Donna, who had already made up her mind not to leave Ontario anyway. Of course she knew even before he had told her but she never mentioned it to him in any of their discussions. Anyway after he told her of the results of the interview and of the offer, she asked if he wanted to go and in truth he said that it was so far away from everything and everyone they knew.

"Great" was her reply and said "then we are staying" He remembered her contented smile. The children had begun their schooling and the west is still too backward for they do not have the Montessori school system out there as yet. It was too much to give up for the amount of salary increase he was offered. Well Don sent back a rejection reply, which provoked a really terse and aggressive response from the Lancashire Medical Director. This response was so savage that it simply justified his decision not to take the job for the reason he had determined.

He smiled as he lay on the bed staring up at the ceiling and was fully awake. He could never understand why these little 'Lord Fauntleroy's' who had built up their little empires just could not enjoy the privilege of their position but rather got the ire of everyone against them, including their medical colleagues. They intimidated their Lab staff and were often found shouting at them with very little feelings for what damage they were doing to the individuals. It is for that reason many of these little tyrants hired the Chief Technical Scientists from the old country.

They thought that the Lab Managers from the old country were better trained. They also projected the fact and philosophy and these managers main job was to train the locals.

But Don had met some of these fellow Brits and many were badly organised, some lazy while others were here to make enough money to return home, to the UK and its quality of life style. There is no doubt that quite a few had been responsible for the growth of the profession by becoming teachers, administrators of the College system and many ran the provincial societies which were the professional bodies. In some ways this also became the "British Mafia Group," which many of the home-grown workers felt was unfair. Many of the home grown were not able to enter the system until after quite a number of years.

This country was very good to them, Don comforted himself with all the inside 'politicking' he had learned how to 'bob and weave' through the system without offending too many. Of course there were always a few who would sort you out anyway but thankfully they were few. He was in his forty-second year and at times he thought that he was lucky to be that age, especially as he was free of any chronic illness. His daughters were doing well and appeared to be well mannered and actually were a treat to take anywhere.

He was cognoscent of the fact that nothing was really given to him and Donna for they had literally worked their respective 'buts off' as in the colloquial expression to achieve all they had. Donna was a good Scientific Worker and had a lot to offer as she moved from full time to part time employment when the children were young. This was a temporary change for she went ot full time employment later on. Such generosity of job movement would not have been possible if she had continued to work in the hospital system. However, she was allowed to have this type of arrangement because she worked in the private medical laboratory sector. Still lying awake his thoughts, Don's mind was flowing freely noting that as they both entered into our forties they began to think of taking things easier at work. Donna did what she had to do because the family needed to have the extra income and she enjoyed the job in Haematology as a lab scientist. She did not particularly like cleaning the house and doing the laundry, so Don had made arrangements to have a house cleaner come in once a week to do a thorough once over the house and to do one major laundry wash.

Donna grew to like this luxury, which was a topic of conversation with some of the other wives. Don had given up gardening as a form of exercise and a potential hobby because it became a necessity. His fixation to have things in order placed an added strain on this domestic task and it took on the same proportions as his strenuous job.

Luckily as he was going through this ambivalence to all things domestic, he was approached by one of the older European porters of the hospital, one by the name of Felix. He had seen this tall porter come into the lab on many occasions and he was always cordial to him smiling and at times taking the time to show Felix what was under the microscope. Felix asked if he could come and look after the garden since he had reached the magic age of sixty-five and he was asked to retire. Don had an interesting relationship with this man, whose hobby was collecting rock encased Trilobites from a site which only he knew. So he would clean and polish these specimens and bring them in to be examined under the plate microscope. Don was interested but only in an academic way but he learned a lot from this working class man, who was intense about his hobby as he was about his other hobby of wood carving.

With all these domestic rearrangements taking place, both Don and Donna had to work to pay for all of these luxuries, considered by some but now a necessity to them and their emerging life style. The possibility of moving to other greener pastures had passed his way and the thought was always there. However, as they crossed over the magic fortieth birthdays, the attraction began to lose some of the lustre. Besides moving from one institution to another to do the same job was not worth it and he had found that to change careers now was too difficult. He was a well-known Microbiologist by his lectures and publications and this reputation was growing. No way could he go to another profession and do as well. At least, that was what he had thought since he had always wanted to be a 'laboratory man,' who was known to be a very practical professional. This outlook transferred to almost every aspect of his profession based on the philosophy that they did if one did not intern from young and over a respectable period of time one could not possibly be any good at anything that one did, certainly one could not call oneself a professional.

Breakthrough into his sojourn:
"Donna, I swear I can hear the girls' voices in the family room" he said to the now tossing figure next to him. "Don't tell me that they are up so early watching television?

Why do you not settle down and have another sleep, you are just hearing things," came the sleepy reply.

"I cannot sleep anymore" he replied. What did I do yesterday after work? he thought to himself. Ah! Yes he remembered how the fellow chiefs came together in the Interns Lounge on the Friday after work and told jokes and had a beer or two. It was a wonderful Friday after work practice which became a ritual. Actually there was some good for the lab chaps at these social sessions where they met the clinical chiefs in a relaxed situation. The medical chiefs also used these sessions to pass along 'thanks' for the laboratory response to assisting in their diagnosis on their specific patient. So much casual education was passed along informally as many clinical difficulties were explained and clinical and pathology scientists had an opportunity to share their problems and solutions.

He recalled as he lay in bed that they were laughing their heads off at the old Director who insisted that he have hard wood benches in the new laboratory. H said that he would have the technical staff rub linseed oil over its surface every day after work. Don's repartees of having the technical staff doing it twice on Saturdays brought renewed gales of laughter. There was lots of fun about the use of formica and granite tops for benches as the whole lab had been brought up to modern standards.

"I do not believe in these new synthetic materials m'boy, for they have sharp edges, which is a risk to the young ladies for they will get their nylons torn" the old Brit broke off in loud laughter "Ho...ho..Ho.. Ho," was his response.

Don could not leave well alone and interrupted him with "Oh! That's all right then since all your staff, are females, you could add a line in your inventory 'Nylons' and have them replaced as they are torn." He would not concede and replied quite soberly; "for now that may be OK but when I leave the new head may hire males." That was the maximum of long range planning considerations given by this man who kept the staff waiting for twelve years to have this lab rebuilt.

As the Friday night 'transfusion' occasion in the interns lounge was coming to an end, Don saw one of the female technologists arrive, so he offered to buy her a beer. She refused and whispered that his wife had just called to remind him to bring home some red wine for supper. He had completely forgotten and returned to say "Sorry guys; I gotta go we are having guests over for supper tonight". Needless to say, that there were lots of 'guy derogatory comments' as he left them. Don did collect the wine and went home. Of course he was not present to assist with the meal so before his breath could be smelt with the fumes of beer, he offered to set the table right away from the missus in the kitchen.

When he went into the kitchen Don looked over Donna's shoulder and asked what was for dessert. She proudly showed him a large trifle. He asked if she had put in sherry but remembered that the evening before she had taken the sherry from the bar cart in the sun room. At the time she remarked that he should replace a new bottle for she was going to use all of what was left.

Don and Donna's guests invariably brought a bottle of wine and recently they were in the habit of bringing two bottles of wine, one white and one red. It was a great evening and it explained why they were still sleepy at seven thirty in the morning. They were in the habit of getting up at five forty five on mornings during the work week. It was the usual winning meal of roast beef, scotches to begin with several glasses of wine with the main meal. The sherry trifle was also a hit followed by brandies and liqueurs with coffee. This usually had the Saturday effect and this morning was no different. The previous week of trials and tribulations and difficult people had all been forgotten.

Don knew that his head was stable while he was lying down but it would not be so if he got up too early. He also felt that if he turned onto his side his brains would pour out of his ear or so it felt. As a result he continued to become drowsy and to doze off again. He thought that he could hear the giggles of the girls who tended to sleep in as well on Saturdays. He and Donna felt quite happy with the sounds coming from the area of the Family room, hearing the girls' laughter distinctly. It seemed as if they lying in bed could almost share in their happiness. As they listened, Don lay back on his pillow and relaxed closing his eyes. A glow of total relaxation appeared to flow over both of them and they put it all down to the booze, which was still present in their systems. The girls' giggling appear to become louder and in some way it appeared to come from their bed head board suddenly. It came so loud and immediate that they both sat up suddenly with a start. It was if the girls were in the room giggling so loudly but it was just the two of them.

AWAKENED:

Then just as quickly the sound disappeared to a gurgle in the next room which was the family room. They looked at each other and jumped out of the bed and rushed into the corridor leading from their bed room past the girl's rooms, which showed empty beds with their usual strewn blankets on the floor. This was the expected morning disarray as they continued towards the family room. Don looked at the clock in the corridor and noted that it was only ten minutes past seven. Don said to the rapidly walking Donna, "Really these kids are watching TV too early" as he stooped to pick up some of their stuffed toys which were lying on the floor. It was then that he heard a shriek.

He rushed into the room to find Donna standing in the doorway as though she was paralysed for she was staring through the picture window of the family room. He looked up and followed her eyes at what she was staring at wide mouthed, through the small covered patio attached to the family room. There were the two girls still in their pjs floating in the air. The patio appeared to be enclosed by a glass bubble.

They had the biggest smiles and were focussed in front of them and away from the house. They looked like gold fishes in a glass bowl. As both Don and Donna automatically moved towards the large picture window they could see a third figure standing in front of the floating girls. It was a slim figure with a silver blue fitted jump suit. The figure was giving the girls some instructions and they were laughing and intently focussed on the person. Both Don and Donna rushed outside and began to bang on the bubble but in spite of the transparent nature of the bubble the girls did not look at them immediately but slowly turned around and looked at them and waved but continued with whatever game was being played. Quite distraught both parents began to shout and bang on the bubble but still there was no response from either the third figure or the girls.

STRANGERS AT DAWN

Don and Donna had rushed out of the sun room still in their night wear, around the containment bubble and could find no entrance. Don said "Maybe there is an entrance from above I will climb on the rail and have a look". Donna stopped shouting immediately and appeared to be concentrating on the adult figure in the middle of the bubble staring at and directing the girls. As she stopped moving and just looked at the figure in the silver suit, Don came and stood next to her. Suddenly a voice came from behind them from the entrance of the French doors out of which they had run from the house "There is no opening" came a soft voice.

They turned around quickly to see a second figure clad like the individual who was in with the girls standing in the doorway. The figure had no obvious face since the clothing appeared to cover the whole body but there were eye openings which looked like the 'cut out' of a Halloween mask. The eyes appeared to be large and brown but they were gentle and appeared to be smiling. Where the nose would have been was a slight elevation of the mask and no obvious outer nares that could be discerned through the masking clothes that covered the entire body.

"Who the hell are you?" shouted Donna. "Get my children out of that dome thing, now."

"Settle down Donna, the girls do not seem to be in any harm, are they?" The voice was not that of Don but of the second being standing in front of them. It continued with its soft and lilting tone, "The children are safe" Both Don and Donna stood closer to each other and to the second clad figure, which was standing in front of them and they felt almost paralysed to make any sudden moves. It was a much shorter man-like figure. It was then Don realised that the 'Being' in front of them did not have a mouth. They were hearing inside their heads which was unusual but not unpleasant and non-threatening in a way. Don tried to speak but found he was whispering, "How are you speaking? " He formed the question in his head and asked the figure.

"My name is Toros. You are taking part in telepathic communication. Do not use your vocal cords. Just think of what you want to say to us and we shall reply in your mind. It is easier. Yes we are from outside of your galaxy," The quiet explanation was given before they could ask. "Are you aliens?" asked Donna with a tremor on her lips. "Maybe you are the aliens but 'yes' to your question" came the quiet reply again in their heads, a bit of ironic humour. "I want my children back" sobbed Donna.

"The bubble is sound proof from the outside so the children cannot hear you and they cannot hear the communication, which we are having. It has enough of the atmosphere so they can breathe easily ... without difficulty. 'The Instructor' has a need for a different mixture of breathing gases that is why the bubble is present," was the quiet reply which, continued "Of course, you can have your children back. Calm yourself! We are not vandals or robbers and do not intend to hurt anyone especially not the children. They are priceless beings in this universe," the calming words of speech came into their heads.

"How do the children come out?" asked the shaken Donna. Don was holding onto her arm and was very close to the 'Being' who was non-threatening and he felt quite calm. He was more curious than frightened. "Yes, how can one enter into the bubble?" he heard himself mentally form the question.

"There are several entrances or openings, which are made but only by the individuals from the inside, beckon to your younger daughter to come to you" was the soft reply. Don could feel Donna trembling although, he appeared to be a quieter person he could sense that she was becoming distraught. Donna went towards the bubble which now felt like a soft plastic.

As if by some unseen instruction, Ellen turned her head towards them smiling. Donna beckoned with her hand to come. Ellen turned completely around and floated towards them with a huge smile and walked through the wall of the bubble and into her mother's arms."Hello Mummy, Daddy" And with open arms she raised up her face to be kissed."Isn't it neat?" We just woke up rushed outside and walked into the magic balloon," she laughingly said. Donna hugged her closely towards her chest and raised her up like a baby. "Are you OK baby?" asked the calmer Donna. "Oh! Yes Mum. When we woke up the magic bubble seemed to call us, Mum. The Instructor has showed us how to speak without using our mouths. Is it ever neat," Ellen continued.

"I have to go back inside now. Bye," and before her parents could hold her, she slid out of Donna's arms and re entered the balloon. Both Don and Donna tried to follow but felt the pressure of the transparent wall force them back..."How can we get in?" They turned to ask in a panic of Toros. By this time they did not seem capable of controlling their voices.

Again the quiet soothing voice in their heads appeared to respond before they could form any question and appeared to anticipate their question. "Close your eyes, Don and Donna" They did as they were told instantly."You will have to become accustomed to the weightless atmosphere within the balloon. Just imagine that you are on a roller coaster and hold onto each other."

They felt as though they had lifted off the ground. Don held onto Donna tightly who had a damaged ear and her balance was not as good as his. Again the buzzing sound in their ear "now walk forward with your eyes closed" was the simple instruction. They just did as they were told and for some unknown reason they both appeared to become very relaxed. Don felt as though he was about to smile, and in fact he was actually smiling.

As though by some magic wand they were floating about two feet off the ground but they were in the balloon. "Hi Dad!" shouted Elizabeth. "Meet our friend the Instructor" as Elizabeth moved immediately between both of them hugging their waists, looking and smiling up at them for she had lowered herself to their height. Don and Donna just held onto her for contact to begin with but also for stabilizing themselves. They turned around to meet the first 'Being' whom they had first seen in the bubble. Don was still in his pyjamas and Donna in her nighties and they felt a bit incongruous but Don stuck out his hand and heard himself say within his head "How do you do?" Donna still holding onto Elizabeth automatically stuck out her hand. Both their hands were held by a very slim small hand of the one called the Instructor. "How do you do Sir, Madam" spoke the very formal soft lilting voice in their heads. They could see Toros standing outside the bubble looking away with his back towards them.

Don found himself asking the Instructor. "How are we standing off the ground? Is there no gravity in here?" Both Don and Donna had frozen grins on their faces. "How can we float up straight? Is this called weightlessness?" Don's questions were in full flow.

"There is very little gravity in here; just enough for you to control your position" came the simple explanation from the Instructor, who continued "can I continue my chat with the children, Sir, Madam?"

They both heard themselves say simultaneously "certainly" and they moved towards the wall of the balloon and were extruded with a slight jerk and found themselves standing outside the balloon next to Toros, who had turned around and reached out to stabilize their return to the firm ground, for they would have certainly fallen down on the ground. Donna found that she was holding down her nighties close to herself as if to preserve and to protect some modesty. It was almost humorous for they were both looking very dishevelled.

Don turned towards Toros and formed the next statement "Donna does not stand heights too well. Her ear was damaged when she was young" he seemed to stutter out as if to form some sort of explanation. It had nothing to do with this scene in their backyard. It was still an early summer morning and no one in their neighbourhood would be up. "Yes, I can see that her cochlea is damaged maybe from the intervention by your 'surgery' not by the childhood infection" came the reply from Toros.

They were all facing the balloon with the girls still looking intently at the Instructor and still floating around but closer to the ground. Elizabeth curls were rising up over her head and Ellen's straight hair just had the ends curled up as by a small breeze. They were in their children's pyjamas which had the Disney characters printed all over them. They looked so pretty, as they always do when they awoke in the morning. Both Don and Donna felt as though they were both thinking about the same things at the same time and appeared to be agreeing with each other. They were actually communicating silently with each other but telepathically.

Don turned to the silent slight figure which he had begun to surreptitiously inspect closely and asked "Where are you from? You are not from Earth" was his rhetoric statement. "We do not have any known living other beings in our galaxy" continued the inquisitive Don.

Donna appeared to be listening to the conversation, while keeping her eyes on the girls and the Instructor in the bubble. She looked quickly around at Don who was facing Toros and nodded in agreement with Don's questions.

"Yes," replied a thoughtful Toros. "We are from a distant galaxy several light years away, that is by your earth measurement" Toros matter of factly communicated." We are called the Omni and I am known as 'The Guide.' My companion is called 'The Instructor.' "

Toros stopped communicating and appeared to be thoughtful He slipped his hands into a slit on the top part of his full tunic as though reaching into his breast pocket but his suit was fitted so tightly to his body. Non-the less, a slit was present and his gloved hand slipped into it. He withdrew two flat silver plates and reached over to Donna placing one on each side of Donna's face. She still had that sort of grin mask on her face. It was if she was uncomfortable and there was some fright which all combined to show acute nervousness. She did not move as Toros, 'The Guide' placed the plates on both sides of her face to cover her ears. She just closed her eyes after about thirty seconds to a minute. Don was watching this little act quite dispassionately; then, the Guide removed his hands with the plates and tucked them back into the slit in his vest suit. Donna opened her eyes and with a big smile said loudly in speech "Oh my gosh! What a sensation! I feel a bit giddy. I think we should go inside and sit down" She was smiling and Don held onto her arm and said "Are you all right you look a bit flushed, love."

"Oh I feel great," she smiled and the strain which was on her face just a few minutes ago was replaced with a calmer face and the radiant disposition which was the norm for her. "What did you do?" Don turned around to face Toros who appeared to be looking intently at Donna.

Toros replied "Donna; you will be all right in a few minutes. You will feel a tingle in your head as the nerves which were damaged in

126

your ear are rejoined together. Your mastoid bone will also grow back in a few weeks."

"What are saying?" Don said startled, joyous but confused. Donna was also staring with a great big smile on her face. 'If what you say is true that would be utterly amazing since our surgeons and physicians said that some surgery could reconstruct the ear drum but that there would always be scarring on the mastoid bone of the inner ear. The nerves were damaged and there was little our medicine could do at this time."

Don looked at Donna again and back to Toros, who because of the covering on his face showed no change in his demeanour. Don stretched out his hand to Toros, who looked down at it and placed his fingers which was also gloved and held Don's finger tips. It was not a hand shake and Don realised that Toros probably did not know this type of greeting but obviously had some sort of version of it. In this instance it was holding onto his finger tips. Don's inquisitive brain was stimulated and so was the calmer Donna as both their scientific minds kicked in and the outcome was pure medical and scientific curiosity. "How did you know all that about Donna's ear problems by just looking at her? How did those plates work? Why did you feel it was necessary to heal her? What are the side effects of your plates?" the roll of questions just appeared to come into both Don and Donna's minds.

"Slowly," responded Toros. They became quiet and calmer suddenly. Both Don and Donna were glancing at the girls from time to time. They had stopped jumping around and appeared to be in some sort of communication with the Instructor looking intently as they do with their teachers at school. The couple now focussed on Toros as they stood next to each other looking over Toros shoulder at the bubble behind him.

Toros looked at them and responded "These 'Shells' are charged and Interphased directly to my nervous system Hence, when it is exposed to another nervous system, it reads and translates, then relates to me all the information of the foreign body. It is up to me if I wish to make a joining with the foreign body. I then transmit my demands through my nervous system to make the damaged tissue whole or repaired. The shells or Plates use my nervous system to get the specifications" stated the soft tones in their heads or minds as Toros replied to their questions. They could not describe how they were communicating but they were aware that they were also cross communicating with each other and for some unknown reason a relaxed atmosphere was forming and much of their apprehension was being dissipated and replaced with a calmer feeling.

"Can I see your 'Shells', Toros. Can I touch them?" asked the now curious Don. "Yes you can see the 'Shells' and yes you can touch them. But, Don they will only work for me, not every Omni has these with them. The 'Shells' are only given to a few. If another Omni or alien were to take them or misplace them, so that some other being was to find them. They will not respond but will self destruct quietly," replied Toros.

Toros replaced his hands into his vest and brought out the Shells but he held on to one end of them so that Don could feel them and turn them over but he never gave up control to Don, who understood why this was so. Don looked up at the figure next to him and said "Toros we see gadgets like these on science fiction films portraying the future as visitors from another planet."

He continued "Look here Toros, I still want to know who you are? why are you here? Won't you be seen by the neighbours? why ...?".

He was interrupted by the raised hand of Toros who when Don was silent said "Sorry Sir, let us take your wife's suggestion and sit down in your garden. I will try to explain as much as possible. Right now you both have a need for sustenance or nourishment. He took out of his upper inside pocket from the same slit where he kept the Shells two small oval pills. Swallow these with some water."

"What are these?" asked the suspicious Don. The Guide explains that the pills contain all the growth and nourishment factors that human bodies require for healthy living except for water. He continued that they will not feel the need for engulfing large amounts of animal and plant tissues for the next earth week or longer.

"What are the side effects on us?" asked Donna. "How do you know what our bodies can tolerate of your concentrated food matter in this pill?" she continued. After a pause the Guide looked at both of them "maybe I did not explain it thoroughly to you both. We have used the same source of food from your planet to make this concentrate so that it suits your earthly bodies. Both the Instructor and I have a different extract." He continued quite seriously but where his mouth should have been there was not even a slit. They could hear and were both thinking of what they wanted to say but they could hear what each other was thinking or about to ask. "The other Omni, who have visited your planet before, were the first to use your vegetation to make the pill to match your physiological requirements and we were issued this stock for you."

Don caught onto this last statement and asked "Excuse me but you mean that you have been observing us earthlings for a long time?"

"Yes," said The Guide "That is our job. But first let me answer your initial question. On our planet many years ago, we have dispensed with your type of food and have mastered the science of concentrating the important elements of life along with the accompanying slow release of nutrients as the body may require. This became necessary five centuries ago when we began to travel across galaxies. Our bodies do not harbour the 'uni-cellular organisms' which you require to break down your heavy dietary food source. In fact we have harboured our uni cellular microbes to work for us and they are not distributed throughout the environment of our world. We must protect ourselves from your microbes meticulously lest we contaminate our transporter and other Omni. I will explain all of this since you are both scientists and are engaged with the fundamentals of this type of Biology"

As though by some silent command Donna got up and went into the house and returned with two glasses of water. Both Don and Donna looked at each other smiled, raised their glasses as though doing a toast popped the pills into their mouths and drank the whole glass of water. When they looked into the 'bubble' the girls were looking at the Instructor intently with bright smiles on their young faces. The Guide did not drink and Don went over and brought over two patio chairs. They were still dressed in their pyjamas and were facing the visitor called Toros or The Guide whose back was against the bubble. This allowed both Don and Donna to keep an eye on the girls and to observe the Instructor.

They could not hear or tune in on what the girls were doing inside the bubble but it all appeared as though they were quite safe and enjoying themselves. They both faced the Guide in front of them with the same intentness as the girls. They felt relaxed and felt no fear, rather there was an intense curiosity as their scientific minds took over. Before they could form any questions in their minds, Toros said to them "listen to our reason for being here and all of your questions will be answered."

He began as though he was about to tell them nursery rhyme"your neighbours and surrounding folks will remain asleep longer today. We are all surrounded by a fog which we have caused to happen. They will not be hurt, in fact they will have the best sleep that they have ever had. They will be in a sleep deeper than they have ever been and this will make them very rested."

At this stage they saw the Instructor take out a sort of game board and showed it to the girls then all three sat on the base of the sphere and began to concentrate. It looked harmless enough for Donna got up went over to peer at them as they were still concentrating and no one looked up at her, when she went and leaned on the bubble. She returned to her seat The Guide raised his hand and they began to focus on him "You were chosen by our pioneer Omni as are other families on your planet, (excuse me) Earth, who are having a similar visit by another Guide and Instructor" Don picked up an as if by a reflex action and interrupted asking "What do you mean by 'chosen' and by whom, he asked forcefully. Donna quieted him in a calm whisper "Let us hear him out. He will explain everything to us and then we will ask all of your questions"

Don looked over at his wife and then to Toros. Toros continued "Thank you Donna. To answer your question Sir, actually you chose yourselves. For we have heard that you have reservations about the educational systems and you have had some discussions with your friends as to how to better educate your children. It is for that reason that we are here. We know that you are the correct persons to offer our services, since you have already accepted so many unknowns such as 'that you are communicating now to 'off worlders or aliens' , 'the bubble', 'the food source' 'this form of communication' 'the Shells' and all of this has been done without primitive anger or suspicion ....not much anyway."

If ever there was a hint of humour this last statement and pause appeared to be it. Both Don and Donna looked at each other and smiled but soon became attentive again. "You asked for a better education for your children and we heard you. On our planet many centuries ago when we began to travel we collected much knowledge and information of other life forms. We have never intervened or tampered with their civilizations or their evolution. Earth has been one such planet which has evolved more rapidly than expected and we believed that there were some other 'Beings' in the galaxy who might have intervened and speeded up your evolution. This made us uncomfortable but after a search of several hundreds of your years we have not been able to find any other life form, which would be capable of doing such a thing. As a result the decision was taken by our Planetary Leadership that we should be a source of some assistance to other civilizations since we did not meet any civilizations as advanced as ours. Our decision to participate at a cosmic level was that we should take some of the young populace, educate them and reintroduce them back to their societies, so that they would become the leaders of their world. The intent was they would be able to assist their own population in an organised manner.

In fact to advance in Science while keeping an ethical perspective for the population. The future generations of Earth will soon travel outside of this little universe which surrounds you and there must be thoughtful respect for what you will meet."

Toros continued "Our peoples loved this new idea of sharing education and so we have become the Tutors of the Universe under the guidance of an organization of which we are part of a section known as the Space Academy.

At present we have recently returned four such trained individuals back to your planet. They hold positions of high authority which will be useful to your population as you take the great leap to explore outside your Universe. You should also know that throughout the past four hundred years of your planet you have had the assistance of such individuals. They have been responsible for keeping the Earth's population safe from self destruction." At the risk of interrupting this alien being in front of them, Don asked "Who are these individuals? What steps have you taken to insure that they do not become tyrants on Earth? How do you know that you can trust them to do the correct thing?" Again to Don's surprise it was Donna who insisted he calm himself and let the Guide finish.

Don and Donna sat quietly and they could see the brown eyes of their visitor called the Guide.

"Do you mean to say that you have been observing us as some great laboratory experiment and have interfered in our existence without our permission, knowledge or respect for our opinion" asked the alert Don. He was shushed again by Donna, who settled him down as though by some unseen force which must have had an effect on him. Donna got up and moved like a cat towards the bubble and again looked at the children for some unknown reason she thought she knew where this was leading and her maternal instincts came into play. Don looked at her and asked her to come back and sit down. She saw that the girls were engrossed in whatever board game they were playing and were obviously quite happy.

"It is our task to look for replacement students from Earth and at this time the Instructor is evaluating your children to see their suitability as the next to enrol in the Space Academy" related the quiet voice of Toros.

"Come on Toros! Human beings do not voluntarily give up their off spring. If you have really studied our species you would know that we are not like that. We, as a race and species, by and large are inextricably bound to our children, bonded by a powerful emotion, which has nothing to do with intellect" said the terse Don.

"We are aware of all that you have said and this is the first time that we are using this technique of temporary adoption by bringing the parents into the process. We have in the past used the lost child and later found child system. In some cases we have had parents act as adoptive parents who have voluntarily allowed their adopted children to seek out their birth parents so that the family could be re united later. It has taken us a long time to understand your 'emotional parental' attachment. We have not found such an attachment in any of our other interplanetary races who have voluntarily given up their progeny for the advancement of their community but Earth people are different. Your literature used to be a source of wonder to us for you have written a great deal about the 'love attachment.' However about two thousand years ago, some of our scholars began to follow your continued addressing of this emotion and its impact on your civilization, has been almost essential to your development and growth. As a result we have tailor-made our educational support to include this emotion and our philosophy has changed so that we choose the families whose children would be the best candidates to be adopted and educated.

We would like to take your children to be part of this endeavour if they pass the Instructor's review" concluded Toros.

Don was up from his seat with his fist in the air "how dare you be so arrogant and insolent to believe any Earth person would give up their children voluntarily. How dare you, Sir!" He continued to take over with a sort of low key anger but his voice was failing or his thoughts were, for it lacked the conviction which would normally accompany such an emotional outburst. Donna interrupted his mental thoughts which, was a sudden onslaught by touching his shoulder causing Don to sit down and look towards her. When they had sat down again Donna said to Don but was looking at the Guide "Don we are being given an option of having our girls become leaders on Earth only if we believe this preposterous story." She looked directly at Toros and asked "How do we know that all you have said is true?" she used an assertive tone in her questioning.

"I could let you enter my "memory store" so you could check out all that I have told you," came the serious reply. "You can stop the Instructor now, Mr Toros!" was the vicious response from Donna. "I think that you just want us humans to experiment with and you would like us to be volunteers in your weird game to capture our innocent kids. It is not on and if you dare to touch our children it will be over my dead body" concluded the now angry Donna.

At this stage a blast of anger and aggressive resentment came with such a jolt to their minds Toros sat up straight then moved to his feet but began to levitate. A very loud voice entered their minds but was addressing Donna, "Be quiet! Madam!" It was such a commanding tone that they both began to sit down. Don could feel the anger and strong emotion building up in Donna's mind as she turned and stared at the two girls in the glass tank which they continued to call the bubble. Then the quiet lilting voice again interrupted her head and they both turned to face Toros, who quietly said "To answer your questions, no one could see us now and if we wished we could have taken the children from you. We did wake up your children and we also woke you both up so that we could explain all that we have spoken about. It will be difficult for you to lose your children for this short period of time but we promise to be around to assist you both with the temporary loss and to assist you to adjust for the time that they will be away"

Both Don and Donna could feel a fury building up in them since the whole thing looked like a fait acompli and Don rose to his feet to try and rip the masked face from the Guide called Toros but he felt a choking sensation which kept this strong animal response in check and he sat down again. Don looked at Donna whose hands were clasped around the rails of the plastic garden chair. They felt as though they were immobile and some force was keeping them both in check. Then a mass of information came into their heads, "We know how difficult this is for you. We understand how you will suffer to begin with the temporary loss or separation. We are not barbarians and we are not unfeeling 'robots.' We have been exposed to emotions and feelings such as yours but have brought it under control. You are incorrect about how you understand the 'scientific fiction' plays where all aliens have no emotions and are barbarians. Your writers are quite incorrect about how they imagine visitors from other galaxies. It is true that we do not all reproduce in a viviparous way like you do. We gave that up to be born in nurseries for we remove any genetic faults before the young are born."

Toros continues to explain "We donate our genetic material for birth in vitro. Individuality is maintained. We do not have the genetic illness and deformity which, continue in your species. We also have allowed a higher form of understanding without the fault of too much emotion to persist and to blossom. There is no disease in our culture and all genetic related impurities have been removed a long time ago from our species. The last illness in our population occurred over three of your light years ago. Genetic vigour is maintained in much the same way as yours that is by mixing the genes which cause enhancement from our pool or race. We do not intend to use your daughters for any medical manipulation."

Toros continues:

That last comment seemed to have lightened the emotional load on both Don and Donna. They seemed to visibly relax. Toros continued "We do keep an emotional involvement in our progenitor or 'parents' Before we biologically die, cells are taken away stored and later on used to form new individuals of ourselves, so we have an opportunity to see our replacement taking place. We also have the opportunity to interact or as you say 'play' with the clones of ourselves. Surely that is the ultimate in understanding between two beings. Both our mental and emotional forces are reunited in the young offspring, which keep our experiences and knowledge as they continue to advance in the new generation. Again your children will not be used as 'guinea pigs.' They are taken to be educated in our advanced learning centre, where they will be exposed to a wealth of knowledge which you do not have as yet. They will bring back that knowledge to cause a quantum increase in your growth as a species."

Don interrupted "But you will only be equipping them to survive on a planet similar to yours and I do not see how that will help Earth. They will behave and be treated like 'odd-balls' when they return to this society." Don sort of blurted out this last statement but felt as though a force was holding him down. He then realised that this force which had interrupted him was coming from his wife even though she had a relaxed appearance on her face.

Toros calmly replied "I can assure you that the re-introduction into Earth's society and governing body will be done within days of their return"

Donna was determined and persisted "what will we do about their school here and how shall we explain to the authorities? What shall we tell our friends? What....."

Her questions were coming with a trembling voice and a panic tone was being assumed. Again the calm and soft voice of the Guide came to them "you will have to cope with those little details but we shall be of some assistance to you if it's needed"

Don interrupted "Donna you are assuming that the kids are going with these foreign beings, are you ..?." He felt a combined force of both the Guide and his wife stop him cold and then he heard a quiet voice in his head and it was Donna

"Don, I do not think that we have any choice, luv. We did ask for help to cope with the type of education over here since we were brought up elsewhere. This alien being is offering the ultimate education and a future for our children. Anyway if they wanted the children they could have taken them without us knowing. I believe that they are trying to live up to a different standard."

"You do not have much of a choice" replied the soft voice of Toros, the Guide.

He continued, "This will be our fourth and last foray to Earth on behalf of the Academy. That is our quota. Both the Instructor and I will retire to our world to raise our own clones and to document our experiences for the past five hundred of your years into our archives"

"How will our daughters return? And who will be their Guide?" came a frantic reply from both Don and Donna almost simultaneously.

"Oh! We will have to complete this assignment which includes the safe return of your daughters. Our task is to relate to the inhabitants of other planets, to seek out the student candidates, evaluate the students and their family, transport, protect, guide and direct our charges, which become the most precious cargo that anyone can have as an assignment. On Graduation from the Academy, where there will be thousands of Aliens (your term)/ citizens from a multiple of Galaxies across the great Cosmos, all are returned to their respective planets. Upon integration and assimilation into their communities we, the Guides and Instructors return to complete our records to the Faculty of Cosmic Studies. We are then desensitized of some mental and physical abilities because the security of the students and confidentiality which are promised by the Academy to the students must be maintained.

The Academy quietly monitors the growth and development of their Alumni to see if they are assisting in the growth and welfare of their home planets and their peoples. We the employees of the Academy will not remember our students or build any long term attachment since this could be damaging to the essence of the Mission, which our people hold sacred to themselves and the philosophy which is tied to their destiny"

Don felt a surge of enthusiasm as though a curtain had broken down for suddenly he felt he understood what these aliens were doing was worthwhile and he turned around totally in his petty opposition to this golden opportunity for his daughters. "That is fine we will come along with you." He felt the total support coming from Donna, who was also standing next to him and when he glanced in her direction he could see that she was in total agreement with him. "I am prepared to leave the planet with you as is my wife," for he could feel Donna's hands in his as she excitedly squeezed them. The Guide averted his brown eyes from them and moved backwards from them by a few steps and after a brief silence the soft tones entered their heads "I am sorry but you will not be welcomed only the children must come alone. If you are present that will be an obstacle and distraction for the Tutors will not have the total attention of your children."

Then before they could shout or make any opposition, the gentle voice continued "Your physical being will also be the source of distress to the other students. It will also be difficult to prevent your built in prejudices from contaminating the other faculty and alumni. This will defeat the purpose of our primary objective necessary for Intergalactic Co operation & Understanding."

Don found himself mentally shouting "Who are you to judge our open mindedness?" Almost at the same time both he and Donna sat down and sheepishly looked at their visitor. There was no force holding or keeping them in a sitting position. Both stood up, one on each side of the Guide and looked into the bubble and quietly watched the girls and the Instructor, who had a small white box open in its hands.

The girls were engrossed at the apparatus which looked like a bedside clock radio. The difference was the acute intense impression on the faces of the girls. As they were observing the trio at work in the bubble, Don became aware of the sweet song of the Red Cardinal coming from the nearby locust tree, which could be seen on the other side of the glass dome. As he was trying to have a view of the bird's location, they were brought out of their temporary reverie by the sound of the soft voice of the Guide "Here, Don, Donna touch this" and as they turned to look at him, his outstretched hand held a small silver cube. They both looked at the object and simultaneously asked "What is it? What does it do?"

THE PACIFIER

They both automatically reached out to touch the silver glistening cube. "It is called a *Pacifier*, which is the nearest form of translation of its capabilities, in your language." said the Guide. They both touched the little square which could just about fill a normal palm. As if by some magic both girls looked up simultaneously, from their intense concentration and walked over to them. Then with the most gorgeous smiles, they stepped through the bubble and walked over to them and threw their arms around their hips. They bent over to receive their hugs. Don bent over to lift up Elizabeth as Donna picked up Ellen. They snuggled up to them and kisses were exchanged by both parents and daughters.

Don and Donna sat down with the girls on their laps on the plastic garden chairs and looked up to see both the Instructor and Guide looking down at them. Suddenly, before any words or thoughts could be exchanged a buzzing sound in their heads brought this suburban family to attention as they turned to look at the pair of aliens standing before them. "The Pacifier connects your emotional and neurological systems to that of the children for you are the most powerful emotional source at this time of their lives. They will always respond to that 'Call or Touch' of their parents in any part of the Universe. Your touch will surpass time and space for they will always respond to your call or touch."

They were both jolted into some reality as the voice in their head was that of Elizabeth's "Mom, Dad we know that it will be difficult for you to let us go but Ellen and I want to go with these people" The parents were shocked as they looked into the sincere eyes of Elizabeth, who was still hugging her dad and looking earnestly at both of them. Donna bent over to kiss her cheeks and said "Darling do you know what you are saying. Do you really want to go with these strangers into outer space and leave your Mum and Dad?"

"No Mum, we will come back. You and dad have always said to our friends that you always wanted the best for us. We have been chosen from the children's population of the whole Earth to have this opportunity. It is the best learning opportunity for us and we are really lucky to be picked, do you not think so?" spoke the quiet and 'oh so sensible' little girl who was not moving her lips but looking directly at both of them with eyes that were speaking. "We have just taken a test like we do in school" continued the quiet voice of Elizabeth.

Ellen little voice interrupted, "It was like a game, Mum but it was fun as well as a test."

For the first time they heard a different intonation in the telepathic voice and it was from the Instructor "Sir, Madam, it is my task to evaluate at site, the students who are chosen for the Academy. We are just in time to take these children away for already there is some neurological deterioration of the hypothalamus and limbic regions." Turning to the Guide, the Instructor related, "We must inform the Academy search committee that they should make the selection for this species at an earlier age. Mental liquidity is impaired at a very early age by the emotional developmental responses. Already there are some physiological changes in the older of the two children, which our physicians must attend too immediately. She is also in need of a stimulus to the immune system for she is prone to many of these earthly microbial infections. Many of these must be addressed as soon as we enter outer space. It will not take long to cure these imperfections and stimulate her immune system before our arrival at the Academy. The wonderful news is that they both Interphased easily with the *Educator,* as she pointed to the small box.

The Instructor looked at both Don and Donna and pointed to the little box, which looked like a bedside alarm clock and said "this works like your little computer." Don's curiosity perked up as did Donna's and he found himself asking, "Do you mean to say that the children can have reciprocal exchanges with that box?"

The Guide spoke, "It is a little more complicated than a mechanical box or your computer used in your home. It contains all the technical advances of your planet to date. It also has the demographics of atmosphere, minerals, biochemical engineering as well as the biological and psychological knowledge of your world. It can instruct children to do the most complicated physical things, such as how to make one of your rocket projectiles. It will show them how they can get the resources, and then give the instructions as to how it showed be assembled and used from their homes."

"I do not think that this is such a good thing," said Don and he could feel Donna's agreement. "It is just an example" came the quiet reply of the Guide."They will not use your primitive method of assemblage of raw materials, but with training of their mental faculties when in full power, would take the materials needed from the atmosphere of any planet or asteroid if the products are available then begin the development of anything they wish. The 'bubble' as you call it, is a product of your atmosphere and it was made by this 'box'.

Your world is evolving rapidly and at times, a bit too quickly for many mistakes are made, which is wasteful because of lack of emotional and psychological immaturity as well as lack of true planning capability. It is such a waste of energy and it will be even more disastrous for you are about to exploit and use the power of DNA. You need both the philosophers, ethicists, your intellectuals and you do have them, as well as your specialists in the humanities. Of course, there is still the basic need in your society for the exchange of wealth, so your fund managers must also work together, at least until everyone is equal or have equal opportunity. It is essential that the society as a group work as a team to consider all aspects of the research results. The need and choice of how it may wish to implement the knowledge while accomplishing benefits for your peoples. Your leaders are heading for a grave catastrophe with this powerful new resource and tool, if social changes are not manifested soon.

We cannot sit idly, while you work with such resources, so we must assist you by seeding your population with suitable skilled individuals, who would be able to contribute to your pool of expertise. The future of every new generation lies with the offspring or progeny. You have not begun to use this vital part of your future until they are too old.

The psychological, neurological and overall brain development, are not allowed to be focussed with the knowledge requirements necessary to develop the population. It is a distressing waste of the human resource. Your primitive use of the in vivo birth technique is still left to chance even though you have the evidence of the successful use of in vitro fertilization. Again the products are in your hands but you need to have a proper philosophy to make the best use of all available knowledge and resource."

Donna interrupted and asked quietly, "How long has our family been under your observation?" The answer came, "You began the process when your husband wrote an article many years ago on how humans should breed the best of the species. It was written as you say in your language 'facetiously'." Don interrupted loudly verbally, which caught both the aliens and Donna off guard. "I wrote that article for our fledgling newsletter to get the by and large apathetic members of our society to sit up and notice. It was not intended to make any more an impression but rather to get a 'rise' or laugh from the membership."

"Non-the-less your short essay did have a very important message which caught our attention and we thought that it was worthwhile following such individuals as yourself. You were heard on many occasions saying to your friends and colleagues that you wanted the best education for your children" responded the Guide. "I object to this breach of our privacy and family life. Regardless of your supposedly noble intentions our children will not go with you" was the very emotional response from Don, who had a hard set to his jaw. "But we have been looking in on your family for the past twenty years" answered the Instructor. "We would not have come to this home if we were not sure of your willingness and co-operation."

"Well, you are wrong Sir or Madam whatever you are. You are a little too glib with your explanations and answers to our questions. You have shown us some of your technical toys and have not furnished us with any worthwhile evidence of such an Academy or any individual on earth or elsewhere who has gone through the system and are currently contributing to our Earthly development. Our children will not be guinea-pigs to your plans and we shall tell all to our press of your invasion of our human rights" answered the now very angry Don.

"Our presence will never get out for you will not remember any of our conversations if we do not wish you to" stated Toros in a mono tone voice heard in their heads."Sir, I ask that you settle down, please. There is one other family who has agreed to have their children come with the Omni. Your children will not meet them at any time not even at the Academy."

The Instructor then continued slowly as Don sat down for he felt the pressure from Donna to listen. "Sir, your apprehension of your Government Leaders to exploit these skilled children is a real danger that is why we have built in safety checks, which assure that they are never detected. Can you really afford not to have your children be among the leaders of your planet in the future?"

At this stage the Guide took his chance and said, "Sir, we have hundreds of Earth-years of experience doing this job and your apprehensions are the same as have been expressed by your predecessors. We know that we have had the answers to all of the questions which may account for our supposedly 'Glib' explanations."

There was silence as Don placed his right arm around the shoulders of Donna who was hugging the children tightly as they both faced the Guide and the Instructor. They were afraid to think as they both felt naked in front of these polite but persistent Aliens, who were capable of reading their minds.

Don and Donna thought simultaneously "Give us some time to think over your proposition" they asked of their visitors. "We are sorry" said the Instructor, "we do not have any time for you to mull things over. The children will come with us today. We would rather have your understanding and compliance for we felt certain, because of your professions that you would agree. That is why we woke you both up for we could just as easily have taken the children but our new instructions based on a change in policy, were to include the decisions of the parents."

They continued, "Under such conditions with the loss of your children you would have had to go through the trauma of the worst kind with your law enforcement officers, as well as with your friends and neighbours. Showing ourselves to you, gives you the opportunity to prepare plans to remove such complications."

"May I speak to my wife and children without you being present or listening and we will use our vocal communication not your telepathic method?" Don politely asked the Guide, who appeared to be the one in charge. The Interpreter appears to be a female if there were male and female in the Omni. The eyes of the Guide shone through the face mask and one would have thought that they were smiling. It bowed from the waist Japanese style and said "You have our word that we will not listen." They both turned away and re entered the bubble almost instantly. Donna turned around holding the hands of the children close to her and they all entered the house. The whole family of four sat on the large sofa very closely together. Donna was the first to break the silence

"Don what are we to do?" the tears were streaming down her cheeks but there were no sobbing sounds as she clutched the girls tighter to her."Sh..hh..hh, let us think this whole incongruous plan over," Don said. He was interrupted by Elizabeth, who said "Mum, Dad may I speak?

"Sure luv," Donna replied. "Well all of this does concern Ellen and me. We really have no choice but to go with the Omni since they have specific plans which they have been working on before either Ellen or I were born. If they wished, we could just vanish and never see you again". She turned to look at her father "Dad, do not try running out the front door and into the car. I can hear what you are thinking" Don was shocked and said "But they said that they would not listen!" "Dad they are not listening but I can focus like they taught Ellen and me to do, so we can talk to each other without moving our lips, isn't that right Ellen?"

Ellen who was the slender and tiny one held onto her mother's hands and had said little until now, "Yes Liz, and I can also use the telepathic way of reading minds. I learned quicker than Liz. Mum, I do not understand why you and dad are so unhappy with us going to school. You said that if you had the money you would send us to Switzerland to a boarding school. Is not going with the Omni like going to a boarding school in Switzerland? I do not like the idea of going away from home but if Lizzie is with me I will be alright and we will look after each other. Mum, you know it is the right thing to do but you are just sorry to let us leave. It is Dad who has to change his mind and you must make that decision now for we want to go that school, in space"

With that little speech, she slowly removed her hands from her Mum's and moved over to the rail of the couch and placed her hands around her dad's shoulder. "You left your home in the islands many years ago and your Mum, our Grandma was very hurt but she knew that you were doing the right thing. We will be doing the right thing too"

"Children, Liz, Ellen, this is not like taking a boat trip on earth! This is going with some very strange aliens into outer space. You might be used, or be experimented on, you may never see us again and worst we will never know what is going on with you. We will not be present when you are hurt and be able to kiss it better. We will not be there to kiss you to sleep and watch you grow into teenagers and then into young ladies and listen when you have your first date or your first kiss" came a strangled sob from Don.

"Dad listen to yourself it is all about how you and Mum feel. You have always wanted the best for Liz and I. It has all dropped into your or our hands. I can feel that the Omni are very honest and truly intend to educate us so that we shall be better than anyone else when we return and we will come back. As for watching after us Dad, Liz asked how we can contact you for we want to know that you are not unhappy when we have gone and we will be able to use the *Pacifier*. It is better than a phone for you can feel our presence and our feelings at anytime by just touching it. We will be in contact with you continuously and when you close your eyes you will be able to see us in your mind so you will be able to see us grow. You will not imagine us growing but you will actually have a clear vision of our body as it develops. The Pacifier will not work if it is in any one else's hands or if we were to die."

Young Ellen placed their parents into quite a position for they were startled by her lucid interpretation of the situation. Don could not help but laugh and hug his younger daughter "I have often said that you should be a lawyer and you better use that gift in whatever field you decide to study."

"Dad, why would you want to call the police, do you really think that you can contact anyone. The Omni said that everyone around our neighbourhood is asleep and there are no electronic devices that are working. The clock has stopped and the light on the VCR is blinking at twelve" said the assertive Elizabeth. She continued "You wanted to discuss this situation and time is running out. We want to go, right Ellen?"

"Of course, but our parents have to give their permission or we will not go voluntarily I believe that the Omni will take us if not today sometime in the future. We must make a decision" said a bright and smiling Ellen.

The children had taken the decision from both Don and Donna's hands. The parents were feeling a bit better about letting the girls go but Don wanted more assurances so he said he will have a private talk with the Guide, but Donna said that she wanted to be present. At this the girls jumped up and hugged their parents as though they were being allowed to go to a midnight theatre show at an underage. "Great," Ellen said that she will collect her Lammie and Elizabeth went to collect her Kawal. Both of these were stuffed toys which the girls have had from the time they were babies and even at their age they kept these toys under their pillows at night. They even took them on holidays and there are a host of stories about these stuffed toys being misplaced on holidays and how they were found.

First stages of departure:
Before the girls went downstairs Elizabeth turned to face them "You know we will be good students and we already have tuned into the *Educator* which has taught us a great deal such as why there are no other living forms in our galaxy, how planets revolve and Mum, you know how you always wanted to know what Mars. Well it was like I had travelled there in my mind and I know what it is like - I actually saw the planet. We will be able to talk to you by using thought waves as both Ellen and I can do now, right Ellen?"

"We sure can and we can also listen to what you and dad are thinking if we wanted to, of course." replied Ellen. Elizabeth looked at her dad and said "Dad maybe it will be better if you work with the Omni for they can assist you with many of your Microbiological problems and so can you Mum. They do not do sciences like we do on Earth but it will be nice to go to this new school for we shall meet all types of different beings who do not look like us. We were told that many do look like humans but some are quite weird, sorry 'different looking.'"

At this Donna came back to some sort of physical reality and shouted "Stop it Elizabeth! You are afraid of science fiction films like 'Star Wars' and now you feel that you will like to meet these new beings in real life? Anyway you both talk as though we have given our permission. We have not said anything as yet."

At this outburst Don perked up and shouted "Elizabeth, are you being communicated with by telepathy from the Omni outside?"

"No Dad, they promised not to intrude or use their telepathy link to listen or interrupt. They are truly honest beings Dad." Don then carried on "Explain how you are using such adult phrases and are able to tell us what is on Mars and trying to make me deal with the Omni. Explain that to me?" He stood up to look at his young daughter who was standing at the end of the corridor leading to the bedrooms. "I really cannot explain how I am behaving but we definitely learned a great deal from the Instructor and the Educator. I know that I am speaking differently but I am only trying to make you and Mum comfortable with our leaving. With regard to permission, do you really have a choice?"

As if speaking to himself, Don quietly said "Are you not going to miss us? Elizabeth came back into the main family room "Dad of course we are going to miss you, how can you ask that. But we shall be in touch with you from the time we leave so that we will not be lonely. Ellen and I will look after each other and we will comfort each other for we will not be separate, they have promised to keep us together. We will be safe where we are going but it is also very exciting."

"How do you know?" asked the sombre Don. "Oh! I asked the Educator but it has assured us that you will love us even more through the Pacifier and with practice we could be communicating with you almost daily I was told. Distance has no measure when compared with thought travel or communication."

"Do you really believe all this science fiction nonsense Elizabeth? What about your friends? What about your music lessons? Are you not going to miss your birthday parties?" was the question asked by the very distraught Donna. "Not really Mum, let me show you. You remember how I wanted a method of remembering the pieces of music, well I asked the Educator and he showed me how to read and remember what I read permanently. I told it that you liked Beethoven" She went over to the piano and closed her eyes and began on *Fur Elise*. They just could not believe what they were hearing. They saw a form of concentration and physical co ordination which they have only seen in professional artists but here was their daughter Elizabeth doing the same thing in their family room dressed in her Pjs. Don stood up and went towards the French doors, stopped and looked out to where he could see the Aliens, the Omni standing in the bubble with their back towards the house.

"OK how did you do that Elizabeth? You have been trying to play that piece for so many weeks. What has happened?" asked the suspicious father. "I can now visualize the whole piece of music by using my alpha waves or something like that, actually the Educator said that I can place myself into a' hyp nindo' state and recall any piece of music once I have read the music What is interesting is that my fingers will keep up with the interpretation made by my brain's alpha waves."

"Elizabeth that is utter rubbish! You have been hypnotised and have performed on cue for us" said the angry Donna. "Mum, how can you accept what you have just said but not what I have explained to you?" asked the spunky daughter. At this Don interrupted them and asked his daughter "what else can you now do since you have met the Omni, Elizabeth?"

"Since both Ellen and I have been formed from both of you, we can assimilate all of your knowledge by going through the 'hyp nindo' exercises using telepathy. This can only be done with assistance from the *Educator*."

As if worn out by the situation Donna asked "Elizabeth, tell us about the Pacifier."

"I believe that the Pacifier is connected to our brain waves linking our emotions to your emotional and brain waves. When touched by either you or us, it signals our sympathetic nervous systems and we will always respond to the call regardless of the occasion or of the distance and time differences. I also believe it can allow us to communicate regardless of where we are in the universe. It is an extremely powerful tool designed for our human race and under extreme stress can be used in a process called 'trans materialization.' It will not respond to anyone else other than the four of us, it is specific" said the now tired youngster. "We must leave you soon and she went towards her parents and circled their necks with her small arms and held them for a while. Elizabeth and Ellen hurried through to the corridor to collect their toys from their bed rooms and to change

Don and Donna went outside and found the two aliens standing outside the bubble which appeared to be vanishing before their eyes. The Guide was the first to address them "It is time for us to go. What is your decision?" Don and Donna stood next to each other with their hands around each other's waist and said "Teach us how to use the Pacifier. We are also charging you and the rest of the Omni civilization to protect our daughters at the risk of your own lives"

When they touched the object called the Pacifier, there was such a warm and comforting feeling and they closed their eyes. They felt themselves being hugged and opened their eyes to see their daughters hugging them. They were happy as they walked over next to the Omni and immediately the bubble formed behind them. All four entered. Both parents heard Elizabeth say

"Here are a few more facts Dad and Mum The Guide has just told Laura that the Einstein Theory of Relativity is only partially correct. We shall be travelling faster than the speed of light along magnetic paths formed by concentrated stars" she related as the bubble began to rise.

"Do you mean 'black holes" asked the parents. "Yes" came the strong thought into both their minds. The bubble just vaporized high in the sky and the mist lifted.

CONCLUSION

By Don & Donna

It has been over twenty years since our girls left us with the strange aliens called the Omni. We moved immediately from our address and went to another Province. We both got new jobs and we just told our friends and neighbours that the girls were in Switzerland attending boarding and finishing school. We also used the Pacifier sometimes several times a day in the beginning and the use was increased many times. However as with all departures, when we lowered the use, then the girls increased their usage. We thought that this phenomenon was due mainly to make sure that we the parents were doing well, not sick or in need of protection from the Earth's authorities.

Donna's physician could not believe how her ear was so totally healed without a scar or any evidence of there being any damage, which was still present in her case history files. Don enjoyed almost perfect health even as he aged and his happy disposition was unfathomable. He did not ask for any help in his scientific research as he was improving and as is usual after years of research many facts drop into a pattern, which explains itself to the researcher. Hence, the belief that scientists should never really retire for their value comes after they have stored much information, which only their brain and their experience can analyze and bring to some degree of fruition. But in Don's case, it was something to do with altruism and wanting to do all the work by himself.

Don was now sixty two years old and has taken an early retirement. Donna is only just sixty and she continues to work. They made a promise not to mention their children to their new colleagues and they soon let their old friends drift away since not many kept up the correspondence.

They had become a very private family of two, with children attending a European Boarding School. The girls had preferred to live abroad and theoretically loved their life style in Europe so they never returned to visit their home. This story was greatly enhanced by the frequent trips that the couple took to Europe, when they returned with the latest photos of their daughters. The children were always dressed in their school uniforms, some were traditional while others were really different, thanks to the power of the Pacifier and its ability to 'Trans-materialise' The couple had got used to the regular mental communication becoming quite proficient and gaining a high degree of proficiency with reading each other's thoughts as well as using telepathy between themselves.

Donna wants to retire when she is sixty two for that is when the girls will return, they will be twenty eight and twenty six years old and it is also the year of their graduation from the Space Academy.

END

COMMENTS BY OTHER READERS

These stories were reviewed by many friends, book clubs and colleagues in Europe, Canada and the USA. Only first names are used at their request "

"Well written, entertaining and what an imagination! Please keep writing"

Marianne S
Roberta

"These are enjoyable tales brought to life by a vivid description against a colourful, historical and cultural back drop of the Science Fiction"

Linda M. Canada
Calgary AB

"Darryl, you have done it again. Keep the stories coming old man"

Chris J
Colonel & Pharmacist
Canada...

I just completed reading your new book and wish to thank you. This was one of the most interesting and informative books that I have read in a very long time. Thank you so much for allowing me this privilege.

Jeanne B,
Richmond Virginia, USA'

Author's Bio

Darryl Gopaul has published over 130 peer –reviewed publications as well as his 7 novels to date. He lives in London Ontario Canada.